Then Came You

A BRADFORD SISTERS NOVELLA

BECKY WADE

For Connie
God bless!
Becky Wade

I'm grateful to the all-star team of women
who worked with me on this novella.
Editor Charlene Patterson, Cover Designer Jennifer
Zemanek, and super readers Brittany, Beth-Anne,
Tima, and Shelli . . . .
Thank you!

One

Garner's Journal Entry

Sylvie left me today.

When Glenna found out, she drove over with this leather-bound journal in her hands and compassion in her eyes. She encouraged me to write my thoughts and feelings in this journal. With a small, sad smile, she said she hoped that doing so might help me.

Then Willow started to cry. So Glenna picked her up and rocked her and hummed a lullaby I don't know.

I watched them together, my sister and my four-week-old baby, knowing I should feel grateful and comforted by Glenna's support. But I don't feel the way I should. I don't feel any of the normal things. Everything about me is lost. Beneath the numbness that's covering me like a thick fog, only two things are registering.

Devastation.

And panic.

It's ten o'clock at night now. Glenna and my mom, who also came by today to help out, left long ago. Willow's sleeping and I'm alone. Alone and frantic. So I'm going to try writing. I minored in English and received A after A on both research papers and creative writing assignments.

That's not why I'm writing tonight, though— because I need to be decent at something. I'm writing because Glenna said it might help and God knows I need help. I'm desperate to make sense of what's happened to me. If I can use words to do that, then I'm willing to try.

I've loved a lot of people in my life. My parents and Glenna. Grandparents, cousins, friends. But I've never loved anyone the way I love Sylvie Rolland. With every inch of my heart and body and mind, I love her.

We met almost a year ago at a party. When I looked across the living room and saw her standing near the fireplace, my life fractured like a stick broken into two halves. Before. And after.

Sylvie's beautiful. Incredibly so.

Think of the most stunning photograph you've ever seen of the most stunning model. A photograph you had a hard time looking away from. A photograph that captivated you and fascinated you. How you felt looking at that photograph is perhaps one-tenth of what I felt when I caught sight of Sylvie for the first time.

She's slim. Tall. She's confident and very much at ease with her body. That night, she was wearing one of her long, patterned sundresses. She'd parted her long blond hair in the middle so that it fell down both sides of her chest.

I asked my friend who she was, and he told me that her name was Sylvie, that she was French, and that she was a friend of Margo.

Margo waved us over. Sylvie turned her porcelain face in my direction and her blue-eyed gaze affected me like a shockwave. We talked. She told me that she'd graduated from a university in France twelve months before, right around the time I'd been graduating from U-Dub. She was on the first leg of a round-the-world tour financed by her father. She explained that she expected her tour to last for years and that she was traveling with nothing but a hiking backpack.

She's an artist. Her trip was about adventure and independence, but also inspiration. She planned to admire works of art from many different countries and to create paintings of her own along the way.

I was amazed by her bravery. She was so different from anyone I'd ever met that it seemed impossible that she'd entered the ordinary routine of my life in northwest Washington State.

I'm an idiot. Because even as she told me that she didn't plan to stay in Merryweather for long, I was already halfway in love with her.

So on this awful day, I can't even blame her. She told me within ten minutes of meeting me that she would leave.

She was honest. I'm the one who told lies to myself.

Sylvie was sexually experienced. A week after we started dating, she undressed me in her room at the Dorchester B&B. I wanted her with a physical passion that made it hurt to breathe. I still do.

The lies I told myself inside her room at the Dorchester B&B: My Christian upbringing made me overly conservative. No one needed to know. My love for her was pure and real and I wanted to marry her as soon as she'd let me, and all of that justified the sex.

Sylvie was impulsive. A month after we started dating, we were sailing on the Hood Canal when she asked me if I wanted to go swimming. Before I could say no, she stood, stripped her dress over her head, and dove in. She came up laughing. Later, after I'd pulled her back into the boat, I held her cold, wet face in my hands while we kissed.

The lies I told myself on that boat: If she ever left Washington, she'd want me to go with her. I'd find a way to leave Bradford Shipping, the company I'd been raised to inherit, and I'd join her on her trip around the world.

Sylvie took everything lightly. Three months after we started dating, we were eating breakfast in bed together on a Saturday while rain drummed against the roof. "I'm pregnant," she told me in her French accent. Then she looked at me teasingly, almost as if she was challenging me to figure out whether or not she was joking.

I slowly swallowed my bite of pancake and syrup, hoping with everything in me that she was joking. We were both twenty-three. I hadn't spent much time thinking about having kids, but when I had, it had always been something that might happen when I was older, long after I was married.

"Well?" she asked.

"Are you really pregnant?" I remember asking. Even more, I remember the hollow way my heart pounded.

She laughed. "I am."

The reality of our situation moved through me in an agonizing spiral.

She told me she could have the baby or have an abortion. Then she shrugged and took a few more bites of breakfast. She asked me what I wanted to do. I told her I wanted what she wanted. She said it might be fun to be pregnant, but that it was early yet. We didn't have to decide immediately. A lot of early pregnancies ended in miscarriage.

A hundred thoughts spun in my head.

We weren't ready for the responsibility of a baby. We didn't know anything about babies. We weren't even engaged yet. We were completely independent for the first time in our lives and neither of us was ready to give up our freedom. The people at church would judge us. The people in my hometown of Merryweather would never see me the same way again.

My father would be furious, my mother deeply disappointed. My parents raised Glenna and me in church. Many times during my high school and college years, they'd lectured me about the importance of abstinence and the dangers of premarital sex. Already, they disliked Sylvie. A pregnancy would throw fuel on that fire.

I didn't want a baby . . . so was I supposed to

pray for a miscarriage now? Until that moment, *abortion*, *miscarriage*, *pregnancy*, and *fatherhood* weren't words that applied to me.

I haven't eaten another pancake since that day.

The lies I told myself that morning while rain pounded the roof: There was no sense in worrying about a pregnancy at that point. Everything would work out fine.

Sylvie was noncommittal. She chose to have the baby—I think because she viewed pregnancy as a new adventure worth experiencing. However, she refused to talk about marrying me or about what would happen after the baby arrived.

Daily during Sylvie's pregnancy, I told her I loved her. In response, she'd smile or kiss me or run a hand through my hair. But always with an air of sympathy.

The lie I told myself during Sylvie's pregnancy: At least now I can be sure that she'll never leave Merryweather.

Sylvie was independent. When Sylvie started having contractions, I felt stupid and terrified and still 70 percent sure that I didn't want this baby. Sylvie wasn't afraid and she wasn't unsure. She communicated her wishes to the doctors and nurses clearly. Never once did she reach for my hand. She didn't need me.

After they placed the newborn in her arms and the delivery room was mostly quiet, she told me she wanted to name our daughter Willow. I agreed. She insisted I choose her middle name, so I chose Elizabeth, after my mother.

I watched Sylvie sweep her finger down the baby's cheek. She touched Willow with an air of sympathy I recognized.

The lie I told myself in the delivery room: Motherhood will change her.

Sylvie was restless. After we brought Willow home to my apartment, her discontent grew. During the daytime, I had to go to work to support us. Whenever I was home these past four weeks, though, I did everything I could to help Sylvie with Willow.

Even so, Sylvie slipped further and further away from me. She stopped focusing her full attention on me. She stopped giving me her bright, flashing smile. My anxiety multiplied.

The lie I told myself after Willow came home: Sylvie's going through the same emotions a lot of women go through after delivery. She'll get over it.

Then this morning, a Saturday morning, I walked into our bedroom to tell Sylvie that I'd fixed oatmeal for breakfast and found her placing her clothes in her backpack. The sight struck me like a punch to the gut. I struggled to draw breath. Willow lay swaddled in the bassinet beside our bed, beginning to cry.

When I asked Sylvie where she was going, pity creased her forehead. Pity.

"I always told you I wouldn't stay long," she said.

"We have a child together."

She told me that it wouldn't be right to take a baby along on such a long trip. That traveling would be too upsetting for poor Willow.

I fought down panic and told Sylvie that there was no way she could leave Willow with me.

She straightened, patted my chest, and told me I'd make a wonderful father. I tried to explain that Willow couldn't survive without her, without a mother. I tried to tell her how much Willow and I needed her.

"I'll always be Willow's mother," she said. "No matter where I go." She lifted Willow, kissed her head, and handed her to me. She reminded me that she'd already stayed in Washington far longer than she'd planned.

She carried her backpack into the kitchen, where she stopped for a few bites of oatmeal and two sips of coffee. She told me she was going to Canada with some of Margo's friends. That she'd decided to hitch a ride with them just the night before.

The whole time, my body was turning dark. The locks closing. The *Open* sign flipping. I followed her outside, holding Willow against my chest. A van waited at the curb, engine running.

I asked her how I'd contact her. She doesn't believe in technology.

She said she'd write. Or call.

I asked her when. When was she going to call?

She had the nerve to shrug. "Someday."

When Sylvie reached the van, she looked back. She gave me the old, dazzling smile I hadn't seen in weeks. She waved, blew us a kiss, waved again, then climbed into the van. The door shut behind her with a bang.

These are the lies I want to tell myself today: Sylvie will change her mind. Sylvie will miss Willow and me so much that she'll come back.

I'll find a way to convince her to marry me.

However, I no longer have the luxury of telling myself lies.

Here are the truths I don't want to face: My love for Sylvie wasn't enough to hold her. Willow wasn't enough to hold her. I'm twenty-four years old, I work full time at Bradford Shipping, I'm clueless about newborns, and now I'm the only parent Willow has left.

Worse, far worse, this is all my fault. My love for Sylvie cracked my integrity and my common sense.

I can't defend the choices I've made except to say that I loved—that I still love—Sylvie.

CHAPTER

Two

Card from Margaret to Her Daughter, Kathleen

Congratulations on your college graduation, darling. At long last, you can now move back home to Snoqualmie where you belong. I've already put clean sheets on your bed.

Love,
Mother

Phone Message from Kathleen to Her Mother, Margaret

Thanks for driving down and taking me to lunch yesterday after the graduation ceremony. And thanks for the offer to move home. That's nice of you, but I'm going to stick with my plan to stay in Spokane through the summer. Grandpa Burke gave me a big check as a graduation gift, so I'll be able to pay rent on my apartment and pay for groceries and all the rest of my expenses until I find a job.

I've sent my résumé to several companies and have three interviews scheduled, so I hope to have good news to share with you soon. Talk to you later!

Postcard from Kathleen to Her Father, Dillon

Daddy,

Here's another postcard for our collection. The dog on the front wearing sunglasses on the beach pretty well sums up my happy, summertime state of mind. My graduation certificate may as well be my Emancipation Proclamation! What I've been able to see and experience of the world up until this point feels WAY too small.

Nothing against the most excellent Gonzaga University. . . . It's just that it was hard to feel completely free there these past four years, seeing as how Mom picked it for me and seeing as how it's just a four-hour drive from home.

From now on, the choices are all mine!

I'm praying that Estée Lauder in NYC responds to the application I sent with an interview offer.

I love you,
Kathleen

Phone Conversation between Kathleen and Her Friend Rose

ROSE: I'm so sorry about Estée Lauder.

KATHLEEN: My heart dropped into my stomach when I read their polite rejection.

ROSE: It'll happen for you one day with Estée Lauder, I just know it. Remind me again what grade you were in when you read that book about Estée Lauder?

KATHLEEN: Fourth.

ROSE: You wrote a book report on it, right?

KATHLEEN: Right.

ROSE: Well, I have faith that the girl who's studied

everything there is to study about Estée Lauder and her company will one day be offered a job there.

KATHLEEN: I was just really hoping I'd be offered a job there *now*. You know? I was already dreaming about the cute coat I'd buy for the New York winter and trying to figure out how to find a roommate with an apartment near a bagel shop.

ROSE: I'm mourning the cute coat and the bagels.

KATHLEEN: I can hear a "but" in your voice.

ROSE: But I've learned that those of us who just graduated have to take what we can get. It's not like putting *treasurer of a sorority* or *junior class vice president* on a résumé counts for as much as actual job experience. My big dream isn't a nursing job back home in Snoqualmie. But a job in Snoqualmie was what I could get. So here I am.

KATHLEEN: I hear you. I think I was overly optimistic about the job market. I've been looking for work for a month now and I only have one offer to show for it.

ROSE: You've been offered a job? What job? Where? You should have told me this first.

KATHLEEN: The company's called Bradford Shipping. They've offered me a position in their Customer Service Department. You don't think that means I'll be sitting in a cubicle wearing a headset, taking calls from complaining people, do you?

ROSE: No, no! The Customer Service Department sounds very impressive. I'm imagining you sitting in a corner office with your business degree framed on the wall.

KATHLEEN: I don't know. . . .

ROSE: What's keeping you from accepting their offer?

KATHLEEN: Bradford Shipping is headquartered in Shelton and you know how much I want to move somewhere new and different. If I live in Shelton, I'll be even closer to my mom than I've been in Spokane. She'll be able to drop in on me anytime and guilt me into coming home on weekends.

ROSE: How good is the offer?

KATHLEEN: The starting pay is just okay but the job comes with healthcare and dental care.

ROSE: Is Bradford Shipping a strong company?

KATHLEEN: They're the largest Pacific shipping company in America. Their history dates back to the 1800s.

ROSE: Then I say go for it. A starter job is better than no job. You'll climb the ranks at Bradford Shipping in no time.

KATHLEEN: Saying yes feels like settling.

ROSE: It's not settling. You have to begin somewhere. Is your business wardrobe ready to go? I think you should buy a lot of white and pale blue tops to wear under your suit jackets.

KATHLEEN: Really?

ROSE: I love white and pale blue with your strawberry blond hair. And you're keeping your hair long, right?

KATHLEEN: Right. Do you think my freckles are getting darker? I'm worried they're getting darker.

ROSE: It's not like your freckles are orange against milky white skin. Your skin is more of a golden tone and your freckles are only one shade darker.

They're subtle and pretty. They give you a beachy, tanned look.

KATHLEEN: I'd rather have your brown hair and non-freckly skin.

ROSE: Chin up. Take your freckles and your business suits to Bradford Shipping and impress the socks off the people in the Customer Service Department.

Phone Message from Margaret to Her Daughter, Kathleen

I just listened to your message saying that you've decided to accept a job with Bradford Shipping. Really, Kathleen. Your Grandfather Burke has assured me that he's eager to give you a good position at Atlas Aeronautics. Your brother has been very successful there. If you went to work at Atlas, Shane could help you and look after you. Plus, you could live rent-free in your old room.

That seems like the most sensible choice, doesn't it?

Call me back, please.

Phone Message from Kathleen to Her Mother, Margaret

Mom, I don't want to rely on Grandpa's charity. I need to make it on my own. I want to work with people who know me for me, not as Shane's younger sister. I've already taken the job at Bradford Shipping and I think it's going to be awesome.

I'll see you and Shane at the country club for brunch on Saturday.

Phone Message from Kathleen to Her Mother, Margaret

At brunch, you mentioned hiring movers for me. Thanks for the offer, but I'll just rent a U-Haul truck. I don't have that much stuff. A lot of my friends are here attending summer school. They'll help me pack the truck, and then Rose and Henry said they'd meet me at my new apartment in Shelton to help me unload.

Letter from Margaret to Her Daughter, Kathleen

Kathleen,

I'm sending this a few days in advance of your move to Shelton so that you'll have a letter waiting for you in the mailbox at your new apartment. I didn't want you to feel desperately lonely when you arrived.

I saw Dorothy yesterday morning at Bible study, and she told me that Bradford Shipping is privately owned by the wealthy Bradford family. Dominic Bradford is the CEO. He married a socialite from Seattle named Elizabeth and they live together in a historic brick mansion on the outskirts of Merryweather. The house is so historic that it has its own name, Bradfordwood. It sits on two hundred acres and was built by Dominic's ancestor, Frederick Bradford. Apparently Frederick was a railroad titan. He's the one who founded Bradford Shipping.

Dominic and Elizabeth have two children. Garner, who works for Bradford Shipping. And Glenna. They're both around your age.

We spoke with the Bradfords a few years ago, at that gala fundraiser for leukemia we attended in Issaquah. Garner has dark brown hair and pale green eyes. Do you remember him? Glenna has brown hair, too, but she wasn't lucky enough to receive those remarkable eyes.

Now that I think about it, I may have been the only one who spoke with them at the gala.

According to Dorothy, Bradford Shipping once controlled an extremely powerful empire of railroads and then, in more recent years, ships. However, in the last few decades, their fortunes have changed. Dominic has squandered or sold off many of the company's resources and Bradford Shipping is a shadow of what it once was.

I was saddened to hear that Garner had a baby out of wedlock with a French woman not long ago. The French woman subsequently left him with the child.

Ephesians 5:3 reads, ". . . among you there must not be even a hint of sexual immorality, or of any kind of impurity, or of greed, because these are improper for God's holy people."

It's upsetting to think that a young man from an upstanding family could be so easily led astray by sexual immorality. It weighs on me, how much the character of your generation has deteriorated. Your father and I were raised to value purity, modesty, and fidelity.

I think it best that you have nothing to do with

Garner Bradford, should your paths cross in the workplace.

I spoke with your Grandfather Burke just now and he told me to tell you that he'll gladly welcome you to Atlas Aeronautics.

Love to you and all my very best wishes with your new job,
Mother

Phone Conversation between Kathleen and Her Friend Rose

KATHLEEN: I just received a letter from my mom. I'm calling so you can talk me down.

ROSE: Would you like me to serve up the usual?

KATHLEEN: Yes, please. The usual.

ROSE: Your mom's been a single mom to you and Shane since you were kids, and being a single mom is pretty much the hardest job there is.

KATHLEEN: Preach on.

ROSE: After that nightmare with your dad, your

mom may have become just a wee bit overprotective of you and your brother.

KATHLEEN: Just a wee bit?

ROSE: We give her grace.

KATHLEEN: We do?

ROSE: Shane's done every single thing your mom's ever asked of him with a smile on his face, but you, Kathleen, may be just a wee bit headstrong and independent.

KATHLEEN: Just a wee bit?

ROSE: When I met you in the seventh grade, your mom was always trying to redo your barrette. No matter how much she tried to finger comb your hair and refasten your barrette, your hair never would cooperate. And that right there pretty much sums up your difficulties with your mother.

KATHLEEN: Preach on.

ROSE: Underneath your mom's desire to control and her sharp opinions, is a woman who loves you. Also, she's the only mother you have.

KATHLEEN: Thank you.

ROSE: How's that? Better?

KATHLEEN: Much better. I can literally feel my blood pressure lowering.

Phone Message from Kathleen to Her Friend Rose

I just got home from my first day at Bradford Shipping and guess what? My duties include sitting in a cubicle wearing a headset, taking calls from complaining people.

Estée Lauder, take me away!

CHAPTER
Three

Garner's Journal Entry

Two weeks have passed since Sylvie left. I've never been this tired in my life. My head feels like it's full of cotton. My body's shaky. I want to punch something most of the time.

When Willow wakes up in the middle of the night, I feed her and change her. Then I wrap her in her baby blanket, even though I still don't think I'm wrapping her up the right way. Sometimes it feels like hours pass before I can get her back to sleep. Before I know it, she's crying again and we do the whole thing over.

Up until Sylvie left, I thought I was doing my share with Willow. I didn't realize then that I was using a piece of tape to fill a hole in a dam. What I was doing for Willow was much, much too little.

No wonder Sylvie ran.

I wish I could run.

It's four in the morning. I finally got Willow settled a little while ago and collapsed into my own bed. I begged sleep to come, but it wouldn't. When anxiety started to claw me, I got up. Now I'm here, at the kitchen table, hunched over this journal.

People keep telling me to sleep when the baby sleeps. But often, when I finally have an opportunity to sleep, I can't.

The responsibility of keeping a newborn baby alive is heavy. You see mothers in pictures and movies rocking their baby and looking joyful and peaceful. I haven't experienced joy or peace once since I became Willow's only parent.

Stressed? Overwhelmed? Anxious? Yes. Those I feel. All the time.

My mom and Glenna have been coming by when they can, but they have lives of their own. If one of them babysits for two hours, then I still have to cover the other twenty-two hours in every twenty-four-hour day.

Willow is my child. She lives because of my actions, and I'm the one who has to take care of her. I've been trying to educate myself on feedings and diapers and washing bottles and giving baths and pediatricians. It doesn't seem to be helping. I'm totally inadequate for this job.

I keep searching Willow's face for features that look like Sylvie's or mine. I can't find any. Her eyes are gray-blue. She's bald. She looks like every other newborn—awkward and frail.

I'm supposed to love her. However, since the day Willow was born, there's been a valley between what I'm supposed to feel and what I actually feel for her, which fills me with guilt. My primary emotions toward Willow are pity and frustration and worry.

It doesn't help that I miss Sylvie every minute. When I wake up to Willow's cries, the first thing that enters my head is the realization that Sylvie's gone.

Sylvie hasn't called.

Not even once.

Garner's Journal Entry

I've finally found someone to take care of Willow during the day so that I can go back to work. It wasn't easy. Mom and I have been looking for someone since Sylvie left three weeks ago, but Merryweather only has a population of six thousand. There aren't a lot of unemployed nannies to choose from.

I considered looking at day cares in Shelton, where Bradford Shipping is located. But Shelton's twelve miles away. Merryweather is where I grew up. It's small and safe here. This is where I want Willow to spend her days.

In the end, I interviewed three nannies. One's references didn't check out. One I didn't like. One speaks nothing but Russian.

The Russian's name is Valentina Fedorov. She's in her early twenties and newly married. Her husband's job recently brought them to America. That's all I know about Valentina, and I only know that much because the lady who recommended her to my mom told my mom those details.

Every time I asked Valentina a question during the interview, she answered by nodding and gesturing with her hands and speaking Russian. I was about to tell Valentina thanks but no thanks when Willow woke up from her nap. Valentina swept Willow from her bassinet, changed her diaper, and started fixing a bottle. She handled Willow confidently, as if taking care of a baby is the easiest and most natural thing in the world.

What got me, though, was the way she looked

at Willow. Valentina beamed at her. Her eyes were gentle. Her smile was soft. Valentina adores Willow the way that I'm supposed to.

I sat on the couch, watching them together, and was so thankful to Valentina for her help that a lump of emotion burned in my throat. Willow deserves to have someone in her life, taking care of her for hours every day, who adores her.

I hired Valentina, then I ordered a Russian/English translation book. I'm too worn out to care about the language barrier between me and Valentina or how much money Valentina is going to cost me.

I'm not rich. None of the Bradford men have believed in trust funds, my father least of all. I get paid exactly what the other entry-level employees in the financial wing of Bradford Shipping get paid. Valentina's going to cost me more than a third of my income.

Like I said, I'm too worn out to care.

Garner's Journal Entry

I don't think it's an exaggeration to say that Valentina has saved my life. And maybe Willow's.

For the past two weeks, I've left for work each

weekday filled with relief. I know I can trust Valentina. I know she'll take better care of Willow than I can. I know that, until the end of the workday, I'm off baby duty.

It's not as if work's enjoyable right now. It's not. Earnings are down and the atmosphere is tense.

My father is the most determined and driven man I've ever met. Control of the family company would have gone to one of his two older brothers if Dad hadn't fought and scratched his way past them, burning bridges as he went. He ended up with the reins of the business and the deed to Bradfordwood. Despite all his ambition, he's not a good leader. He's unable to trust the people he's hired. He insists on getting his way in everything. He refuses to change with the times.

Our ships are old and inefficient. We need a new fleet, the latest machinery, newer technology, and modern workflow systems in order to compete with West Coast Transporters. However, my father refuses to invest the kind of capital those upgrades would require. So West Coast Transporters has eaten into our market share more and more over the past ten years. Our contracts are down.

I don't like the pressure we're all under or the desperate way everyone's treading water. But these days, when I look at my co-workers, all I can think is that at least there's not a crying baby or a hungry baby or a baby with a fever at the office.

Work is hard. But I have a new perspective on it because I know for certain that taking care of a newborn is harder.

Garner's Journal Entry

Every night, I sit in the rocking chair in the nursery when I give Willow her bedtime bottle. Tonight, I burped her halfway through her feeding like always. Then I sat her on my knees facing me and made funny faces.

She looked right into my eyes. And she smiled.

She's ten weeks old and she just gave me her very first smile. I wish I'd taken a picture. I'm probably supposed to be documenting everything better for her baby book or whatever. She's going to have a terrible baby book.

But at least she'll have a father who loves her. Because when she smiled at me tonight, I finally felt it. Love. A rush of love.

I was so blown away by it I laughed, which made her smile at me even more. Then I hugged her small body and breathed in the smell of her

Johnson's baby shampoo. I could feel her heartbeat.

Up until tonight, I was pretty sure Willow didn't like me, and I understood why she didn't. I didn't blame her for resenting the idiot, bumbling guy who started doing for her all the things her gorgeous, familiar mother had done before.

But tonight . . . tonight my little girl smiled at me. She gave her very first smile to me because I'm her person now.

I'm her daddy and, in her way, I think she might love me, too.

When I laid her against the inside of my elbow to feed her the rest of her bottle, her hand made a fist in the fabric of my shirt. She watched me as she drank down her formula.

I'm tired and lonely. Parenting is far more difficult than I understood when I was a son and not yet a father. I miss my freedom and my friends and the life I had before Sylvie told me she was pregnant. I miss who I used to be.

But tonight my daughter, a tiny girl in pink pajamas, smiled at me. Because I'm her person.

Letter from Sylvie to Garner

Greetings from Canada. I've been staying in an artists' colony for the past two months. It's beautiful here! So peaceful. I've been hiking, canoeing, learning, and creating every day. I am myself again.

I hope all is well with you and that you're not too angry with me. You would never have been happy with me for very long. You're a traditional man and I'm the opposite of that. Be happy, Garner.

Give my love to our *petite cherie*! I hope she enjoys her new dress from her *maman*.

Sylvie

Garner's Journal Entry

I finally received communication from Sylvie. I stood by the apartment complex's wall of mailboxes after work this evening, reading her letter. Anyone who saw me would have seen nothing but stillness. Inside me, though, a bonfire of anger and bitterness and love and need was burning.

The dress Sylvie sent Willow is too small. Sylvie

was here for the first month of Willow's life, but she's been gone for two months now. She's missed two-thirds of Willow's life and already she has no idea what size Willow wears.

I want to kill Sylvie and at the same time I desperately want her to come back and love me.

Letter from Garner to Sylvie

Sylvie,

After taking care of Willow myself, I completely understand why you would've needed a break. I'm glad you feel like yourself again.

Please call me as soon as you have a chance. It's extremely important that we communicate with one another and work out a custody agreement that suits us both.

Garner

Note on the Back of the Above Letter, Which Was Returned to Sender Unopened

Sorry, but you missed Sylvie. She left the artists'

colony four days ago without leaving a forwarding address.

Garner's Journal Entry

I need to accept the fact that Sylvie's never coming back. I know I need to. I can't, though. Maybe I can't because a part of me continues to believe that the Sylvie I loved wouldn't abandon me and Willow like this. Maybe I can't because I'm too selfish to deal with what Sylvie's abandonment means for my life.

A single father . . . without any end in sight? For the next eighteen years until Willow goes away to college?

Dread washes over me whenever I think about it. So I try not to think about it.

I'm still hoping that Sylvie's love for Willow will pull Sylvie back to Washington like a kite on a string that's being wound in and in and in.

Garner's Journal Entry

A kite on a string? Is that really what I wrote? What a load of stupidity.

Sylvie called today. Willow's five months old and this is the first I've heard from Sylvie since the letter.

She kicked off the conversation as if nothing were wrong. Her voice sounded rested and cheerful and listening to it made me remember every detail of her. Her pale blond hair. Her sundresses. Her smell. Her body.

In the background, I could hear people talking, laughing, glasses clinking.

She asked about Willow and I gave her an update, fighting the whole time to sound reasonable, to keep my temper in check. She asked me to hold the phone to Willow's ear so she could talk to her. So I did, but Willow pushed the phone away. She was more interested in the toys on her play mat.

I asked Sylvie when she planned to visit. I knew that pressuring her might cause her to disappear. At the same time, after the way she's treated me, she owes me answers.

"I'm not coming back through Washington," she said.

In the pause that followed, the last of my faith in her crashed to the ground. "Don't wait for me," she told me. "I wouldn't want you to wait, Garner. Go on! Enjoy."

Enjoy.

Enjoy, she said.

I couldn't find words.

She went on to shovel a lot of nonsense about how she's not the type of woman who can be an everyday mother, that she'd rather be an unusual mother than a conventional one. That she'll make it up as she goes.

I told her I needed to know where I could reach her.

She laughed and said she didn't even know where she'd be tomorrow. "Don't worry," she said.

"Don't worry!" I shouted the words.

She assured me that Willow and I would be fine.

I tried again to tell her that I needed to know where I could reach her.

A dial tone answered.

Sylvie would call herself enlightened. I thought that about her once. But she's nothing but selfish and shallow.

She left her baby behind.

I hope that remorse catches up with her one day. And when it does, I hope Sylvie chokes on it.

Garner's Journal Entry

Over and over since Sylvie left, I've asked God to forgive me. I've prayed for forgiveness on my knees at home, at my desk at work, while looking into Willow's eyes.

I know the Bible says that when you ask for forgiveness, God gives it. Only, I don't feel forgiven. I'm having a hard time believing that He's forgiven me. I'm having a hard time forgiving myself.

Every day I understand more fully that for the rest of my life, people will view me as the guy whose sin and gullibility and carelessness resulted in an illegitimate child. That's my new identity.

Maybe because of that, or despite that, or because of all the praying I've been doing, I wanted to go back to church. I hadn't been in more than a year because I'm already the guy whose sin resulted in an illegitimate child at work and around town. I didn't want to have to be that guy at church, too.

But in the end, I missed it too much to stay away.

I carried Willow into the building with all my defenses up. I was ready to turn and leave for any reason. But the people at church surprised me.

They welcomed me like they'd missed me, too. They showed me incredible grace.

It humbled me. It seemed like far better than I deserved.

Less than ten minutes later, I handed Willow to the ladies in the baby nursery. They made a big fuss over her, smiling and praising her and arguing over who'd get to hold her first.

I realized then that I had a whole new reason to appreciate church.

Free childcare.

Garner's Journal Entry

Two things happened this week.

The first thing that happened: Willow turned six months old. The fussy, crying newborn who wouldn't sleep is now a mellow, observant baby who sleeps all night.

Slowly, Willow's gray eyes turned green, like mine. In every other way than that one, the older she gets, the more she looks like Sylvie. Her hair is coming in blond. Her skin is very fair, like Sylvie's. Her little face is perfect.

The resemblance between Sylvie and Willow is a blessing and a curse. A blessing for Willow because she inherited her mother's beauty. A curse for me because Willow's appearance reminds me constantly of Sylvie.

The second thing that happened: I met someone. At church.

Her name's Robin Bowman. It turns out that we were in the same class at U-Dub. She works at a bookstore and dreams of owning her own bookstore one day.

Everything about Robin is different from Sylvie. Her personality. Her values. Her appearance. Robin's several inches shorter than Sylvie and she has light brown hair and brown eyes. Pale pink cheeks. Her smile is shy, but also warm and genuine.

She's nice. It sounds weak, that word. But after Sylvie, I have a fresh appreciation of what nice is worth. Robin looks at me the way women used to look at me. With respect and interest.

I asked her out. Glenna's agreed to watch Willow so I can take Robin to dinner and a movie.

Garner's Journal Entry

I'm surprised to see how long it's been since my last entry. As Glenna predicted, writing in this journal helped me through my worst moments. I was able to order my thoughts by ordering my words.

Since I last wrote, life has been manageable, thanks to Robin. I haven't written because I haven't needed to get my head straight.

Robin is the most thoughtful, helpful, and encouraging girlfriend possible. She doesn't have a mean bone in her body. She's peaceful. Level headed. Normal. She's got her life together. She's as strong in her faith as anyone I've ever met. I can trust her.

Plus, Robin loves Willow and Willow loves Robin. Every time Willow sees Robin, she grins and reaches for her and Robin cuddles her and kisses her neck. I think that God sent Robin to us, in part, because He knew Willow didn't have a mother and He knew what a perfect mother Robin would make.

This time around, with Robin, I'm doing everything right. Robin and I started dating four months ago. We've done nothing to be ashamed of in all that time. And tonight, we got engaged.

My parents approve.

Robin's parents aren't as sure. A man who comes with a baby isn't what they'd have chosen for Robin, who has never once made a bad decision. I think her parents see me as her first bad decision. There's not much I can do about that except hope that I'll be able to win them over in time.

Glenna's skeptical. When I told her I was going to propose, she told me she's concerned that my relationship with Robin is too much, too soon after Sylvie. She thinks I'm on the rebound. I tried to explain to her that Robin was what I needed at exactly the right time.

It's easy to be with Robin. I'm not torn apart by guilt or out of my head with lust or sick to my stomach with fear that she'll leave. She makes me and my life better. She's improved everything. She doesn't come with downsides.

The three of us, Willow and Robin and me, have a bright future.

Garner's Journal Entry

As it turns out, the four of us have a future. I brought out my journal today because Robin told me this morning that she's pregnant. Soon, we'll become a family of four. Willow, the baby, Robin, and me.

Robin and I married a few months ago at our

church, the church where we met. Even before the wedding, Robin told me that she hoped we'd have kids right away. She wanted Willow to have a sister or brother near to her in age. Robin was also eager for her own sake. She wants to be a young mom. She can hardly wait to have this baby.

I'm going to be a father again.

I'm still trying to get my head around it.

It's a big responsibility. Even so, this day feels totally different than the day Sylvie told me she was pregnant. That time, pregnancy seemed like a disaster. This time, it's something to celebrate. This baby is Robin's dream come true.

When Sylvie left and it was my job to keep Willow alive, I couldn't imagine how a newborn could be anyone's dream come true. But when I look at Willow these days, I get it. Willow's fifteen months old. She has big blond curls. She's walking everywhere. She's full of energy and spends all of her time exploring stuff and climbing on stuff and talking. Her first word was, "Dada."

Willow didn't come at the stage of my life I would have chosen. Raising her without her mother wasn't what I'd have chosen, either. But Willow herself? Willow is the light of my life. I love her with fierce, devoted love. Whenever I think about how easily I would have agreed if

Sylvie had decided to get an abortion, a chill plunges through me.

Thank God it didn't go that way. Thank God for Willow and thank God for Robin.

I'm still getting to know my wife.

Robin loves old movies, hot tea, and anything British. She's organized and health conscious. We moved into our first home right after the wedding. It's a three-bedroom, two-bathroom house built in the '50s and Robin keeps it incredibly neat. When I come home from work, the table's set, she's cooked some sort of low-fat dinner for us, and she has at least one vanilla-scented candle burning.

Robin likes structure. During the week, she and Valentina work together to make sure Willow stays on a schedule. On the weekends, Robin and I often rush back from visits to her parents or my parents or the park to make sure Willow's in bed at the right time.

Robin's soft-hearted. She gets teary-eyed over commercials that involve dogs or reunions.

Robin's patient. Sylvie would get mad sometimes. Sylvie and I would fight and slam doors and then make up with tears and kisses. That's not how Robin operates. She's very much in control of her temper. We haven't had a single fight. I'm sure we will fight, eventually. All couples fight. Yet it's hard for me even to picture Robin being furious with me or me being furious with Robin.

I've just glanced back over this journal entry and realized that I've made Robin sound like a saint. She does have a few weaknesses.

I tried to talk her into a honeymoon in England, because she loves Great Britain so much. But I couldn't convince her to go. Travel makes her nervous. So do parties that involve more than ten people. So do big dogs.

She second-guesses herself a lot and often asks me whether I think she did the right thing regarding her friendships, her job, her parenting. Here's the thing. Robin *always* does the right thing. She's one of the best people I've ever known. Her intuition is excellent. It's her confidence that's shaky.

Between her job at the bookstore and Willow and me, she's on her feet most of the day. She's such a high achiever that she'll keep going until she's at the point of exhaustion. She doesn't know when or how to slow down and rest. I've started insisting that she do some things for herself. While we were dating, she loved taking walks for exercise. After we married, she let that go. I've talked her into starting the walks back up again.

That's it. That's everything that's happened.

I'm going to be a father again.

At times, the last two years of my life were like a stormy sea. But from where I'm standing, the sea ahead looks calm and quiet.

CHAPTER

Four

Phone Conversation between Kathleen and Her Friend Rose

KATHLEEN: By the way, I finally, just today, saw Garner Bradford for the first time. Do you remember who he is? The one my mother warns me about all the time?

ROSE: The son of the guy who owns Bradford Shipping?

KATHLEEN: Exactly.

ROSE: I'm surprised this is the first time you've seen him. You've been working for Bradford Shipping for how long now?

KATHLEEN: Two years. Remember, though, the first year, I was stuck wearing a headset and taking orders and murmuring consolingly. I never saw anyone that year. If the President of the United States had dropped in to speak to the employees of the company, I wouldn't have been invited. I was a grunt.

ROSE: Thank goodness you got promoted.

KATHLEEN: To a job assisting the assistant to the head of the Customer Service Department. Our building's on a different part of the campus than the executive offices where Dominic and Garner Bradford work.

ROSE: Ah.

KATHLEEN: I wish we all shared one big building, because then I'd have a chance of handing my reports to Dominic Bradford himself. As it is, I have no way of knowing whether he's received the reports I've sent him.

ROSE: Why wouldn't he be receiving them?

KATHLEEN: One of his secretaries could be intercepting them and passing off my recommendations for improving the company's business model as her own?

ROSE: Nope. That's too far-fetched.

KATHLEEN: One of his secretaries could be intercepting them because she doesn't think he'll be interested or have the time to read them?

ROSE: That, I'll buy. It's also possible that the reports have reached him and that he's read part or all of them but failed to communicate that to you.

KATHLEEN: True.

ROSE: Don't sound so discouraged.

KATHLEEN: Years have passed and I'm no closer to a job at Estée Lauder. My office is so small that I'm unable to fit an office plant into it—

ROSE: At least you *have* an office!

KATHLEEN: —and there's a 50-percent chance that I'll receive a call from my mother at some point today reissuing Grandpa Burke's invitation to work at Atlas Aeronautics. Which, by the way, I'm tempted to accept.

ROSE: No, ma'am.

KATHLEEN: Yes! The pay would be *so* good, Rose. I want better shoes.

ROSE: You are not going to mooch off Grandpa Burke like your mother and brother. You're going to make your own way in the world—you *are* making your own way in the world—just like you always said you would.

KATHLEEN: Fine. Be right all the time.

ROSE: I want to hear more about Garner Bradford. Where were you when you spotted him?

KATHLEEN: Once every quarter on a Friday afternoon, Bradford Shipping holds a barbecue picnic for employees and their families. Garner didn't go to the picnics I attended in the past. But this time, he did.

ROSE: What does he look like?

KATHLEEN: He has light eyes and tanned skin and brown hair. I love that combination, don't you? That olive skin and light eyes thing?

ROSE: I totally love it.

KATHLEEN: Me too. It's rare enough that whenever

I see it, I catch myself staring. Garner's well-built and there's an ... I don't know ... an easy strength about the way he carries himself.

ROSE: It's been a while since your last boyfriend. . . .

KATHLEEN: Garner's married. He was at the picnic with his wife and his two little girls, Willow and Nora. It was so cute, the way he was carrying his two-month-old baby and holding hands with his adorable little blond daughter. While I was on my way over to introduce myself, he went off in another direction. So I ended up talking to his wife, Robin.

ROSE: What's she like?

KATHLEEN: She's soft-spoken and she was so genuinely sweet that she made me feel comfortable right away. I got the sense that she's one of those women who was put on this earth to be a mother.

ROSE: Is she pretty?

KATHLEEN: In an understated, girl-next-door kind of way. Speaking of pretty, have you decided on bridesmaids' dresses for us yet?

ROSE: Well, Henry told me to pick the one that I like best so I think I'm going to go with the pink bridesmaid's dress you tried on at Heidi's.

KATHLEEN: Great!

ROSE: I love pink.

KATHLEEN: You always have, my dear. You're the queen of your wedding day. I agree with Henry, as usual. You should pick the one that you like best.

Phone Message from Margaret to Her Daughter, Kathleen

Darling, this is Mother. Make sure that Rose understands that she can choose any color of bridesmaid's dress except pink. With your hair color, you'll look dreadful in pink.

Also, I hope that she's invited the minister to preach to the congregation during the ceremony. So many Christian women have devalued that part of the service. It's becoming hard to tell a secular wedding from a Christian wedding these days! Rose will have guests in attendance who are non-believers, and a sermon could be very critical to their salvation.

By the way, the furrier called. My mink is ready to be picked up, thank goodness. So I'll be able to wear it to brunch Saturday.

Well. I'm off to attend the knitting circle at church. I can't stand going. I don't knit, for one thing. But the knitters keep putting me on the invitation list and *someone* has to make sure that blankets are knit for babies who might not otherwise have them. "Whatever you do, work at it with all your heart, as working for the Lord, not for human masters . . ." That's Colossians 3:23, Kathleen. Words to live by.

By the way, you really ought to think about going to work for your Grandfather Burke. It's time.

Postcard from Kathleen to Her Father, Dillon

Greetings from NYC!

I'm sitting in a deli eating a phenomenal pastrami on rye and thinking of you. You and I have always liked pastrami on rye.

Mom and Shane think I'm crazy for traveling to New York alone. Just between you and me, it's a little lonelier to travel by myself than I realized it would be. But I've always wanted to see New York in the fall. It's everything I imagined and more. Louder. Bigger. Smellier. Grander. More electric.

The meeting I set up with my contact in the HR Department at Estée Lauder went well, though I have a sneaking suspicion she may just have been humoring me.

Rose and Henry are in Hawaii on their honeymoon. At this moment, they're probably wearing leis, attending a luau, and saying, "Aloha" to everyone. Now that Rose's dream of marriage and family is coming true, I'm trying not to be impatient with God about MY dream.

Aloha,
Kathleen (who's shaking her fist at the ceiling of the deli and shouting, "God! Hurry up!")

p.s. I love you.

Phone Message from Kathleen to Her Friend Rose

Oh, Rose. Remember when I told you about meeting Garner Bradford's nice wife at the company picnic?

Well, the woman who was raped and murdered at Blue Heron Park yesterday, the one they've been talking about on the news . . . It was Robin

Bradford, Garner's wife. She's the one who was raped and murdered. I feel sick to my stomach.

Apparently, the news stations just released the victim's identity. When I got to work, everyone here was in shock over it.

She was so friendly, Rose. I can't get the memory of her and those two little girls, Willow and Nora, out of my mind.

I'm going to hang up and pray. I know that's what you'd tell me to do. I'll pray.

It's . . . It's awful to think about something so vicious happening to someone I've met, someone connected to Bradford Shipping. She was walking in the park for exercise last night when she was attacked. It wasn't even dark out. What happened to her could have just as easily happened to you or me.

Instead it was Robin Bradford and now those girls have lost their mother. The older one's two. The younger one is only seven months old.

Okay. Bye. I'm going to pray.

Call me.

Sheet of Paper Taped to the Door of Kathleen's Apartment

Darling,

I saw on television this morning that the woman murdered at Blue Heron Park was Garner Bradford's wife. I've left several messages for you but I haven't heard back so I decided to drive over. I'll wait for you at the little restaurant around the corner from your apartment that you like. Drive there, and I'll buy you dinner and some of that strawberry pie they're famous for.

Have you heard that they think the man who killed Robin Bradford was the Duct Tape Rapist? If so, Robin is his sixth victim and he's still on the loose. In this very part of Washington.

Don't go walking by yourself. Anywhere! I stopped by the store and bought Mace for you. And one of those alarms for your key ring. And a Swiss Army knife.

This world we live in is a sinful, terrible place. I'm convinced we're living in the end times. I've spent most of the day reading Revelation.

Come straight to the restaurant.

Mother

Phone Conversation between Kathleen and Her Friend Rose

KATHLEEN: Did you hear that they arrested the guy who killed Robin Bradford?

ROSE: No! I hadn't heard. I'm so glad they found him.

KATHLEEN: I know. His name's Brian Raymond. He's thirty years old and he's an engineer with the Department of Transportation.

ROSE: Have they charged him with murder?

KATHLEEN: Yes. I guess evidence from the scene connected Brian to the other Duct Tape Rapist cases because they've charged him with those five rapes as well as Robin's murder.

ROSE: Have you heard how Garner and the girls are doing?

KATHLEEN: The word around the office is that Garner's devastated, but that he's doing his best to take care of the girls. Imagine how confused they must be. They're so young. I feel horribly for him. And them.

CHAPTER

Five

Garner's Journal Entry

I'm living with nightmares. Nightmares meet me
when I sleep and nightmares meet me when I wake
up. I keep wishing I could escape them. But that's a
futile wish.

Robin is dead.

Just writing that makes my stomach tighten
with denial and pain. It's impossible to accept that
this is our reality, even though it's been ten days
since she died. The funeral's done. She's buried in a
coffin with six feet of dirt on top of her, and still, I
can't believe it.

Robin's mouth and wrists were duct-taped.
Then she was raped and strangled. This is the truth
of what happened. To Robin, a woman who was

full of kindness.

I gave the police all the information they asked for during those first sickening and surreal days after her murder. It wasn't much. I'd have liked to have done more, for Robin's sake. The detectives deserve all the credit. They're the ones who studied the evidence, who hunted down Brian Raymond, and who put him behind bars. They did their jobs and moved on.

I can't move on.

How much pain was Robin in? What was going through her mind during the attack? Did she try to call for me from behind the duct tape?

Bile's rising up my throat like it does every time I ask myself these questions. I don't let myself ask them often because when I do, I can't function. I have to be able to function because Willow and Nora need me.

Robin is dead.

This awful thing happened to her, to us. I can't believe it.

I have to believe it.

Garner's Journal Entry

When Sylvie left me with Willow, I didn't know

how to take care of a baby. This time, I know how to feed them, and give them baths, and put them to bed. But I don't know how to help them with their grief. They're traumatized. Both of them cry for Robin.

Nora's a baby and Robin was her anchor. She's too young to talk, but her eyes are filled with fear and vulnerability. She's not sleeping or eating the way that she was for Robin.

Willow wanders around the house, holding her blanket, calling, "Mommy? Mommy!" over and over in a worried voice.

It breaks my heart. Both of them are breaking my heart.

I'm spending all my time with them. I'm doing everything I can to get them through this. I'm loving them with everything I have even though I know it's not enough. I can't be for them what Robin was. No one—not me, not anyone—can replace her. They'll have to grow up with this huge blank space in their lives because their mother, the woman they both depended on and loved, is gone. I'm terrified that Robin's loss will scar the girls in a way that will never heal.

After Nora was born and Robin decided to become a stay-at-home mom, Robin suggested that we let Valentina go. I talked Robin into keeping

Valentina. I told Robin that I wanted her to have help around the house and with the girls. The truth is that I kept Valentina because I owe her. I haven't forgotten how Valentina saved Willow and me.

And now Valentina is saving us all over again. She's been with us every day since Robin died. Shopping. Cooking. Doing laundry. Cleaning. Answering the door when people at church that I can't stand to talk to bring over food. Staying at the house when Nora naps so I can take Willow to the park or to the mall or to the water.

Weekends and weekdays are blurring together. I only know that Valentina has been here every day. Whenever we've needed her, she's been here.

Garner's Journal Entry

My thoughts keep going back to the night Robin was killed.

When I came home from work that night, she was dressed in work-out clothes. She had dinner waiting and she gave me instructions about the girls. When to put them down. Which book Willow wanted before bed. Something about Nora's bottle. Then she kissed me, and smiled, and left. The whole time, she was hurrying to get out the door. I was distracted because Willow was tugging on my hand to get my attention.

I've racked my brain but I can't remember what Robin's last words to me were. Or what mine were to her. I only remember that everything seemed normal.

Those moments weren't normal at all because they were the last moments I'll ever have with Robin. Why can't I remember my last words to her?

I wish I'd known those moments were our last. I wish I'd done everything differently.

Robin ~~goes~~ went walking a lot. Several afternoons a week, almost always with her friend. I hate that I'm the one who encouraged her to make time in her schedule to go walking. I did it with good intentions. But good intentions are worthless in the face of a result this terrible.

I hate that I didn't ask to make sure her friend was going with her that night. If I'd realized that her friend had other plans and that Robin would be walking alone, then I might have suggested that she walk around our neighborhood or drive to Mom and Dad's and walk on Bradfordwood's property.

I hate that I didn't get home earlier that night. If I had, she could have left to go walking earlier.

Maybe then, Brian Raymond would have missed her.

I hate that I didn't pray for her safety that day, that I took her safety for granted. That's a mistake I'll never make again, not with anyone I love.

I wish I'd thanked her or told her what a great mom she was or said how much we cared about her.

But I didn't.

I have a thousand regrets.

Garner's Journal Entry

Sometimes, I'm furious with God.

Robin trusted God fully, and look where that got her. God should have honored her faith in Him by keeping her safe when she needed Him most.

So, yes. Sometimes I'm furious. The rest of the time, though, I'm aware that God was the one who was with her at the end. He was the one who made sure her soul didn't die forever on that muddy stretch of grass.

I haven't been the best Christian all my life. But I am certain that God swept Robin away from the pain and the terror of her final moments and brought her to a place of joy and peace.

That certainty is the only thing that allows me to sleep at night.

Garner's Journal Entry

Guilt is like a cancer.

I'm terrified that Glenna was right, back when I told her I was going to propose to Robin and she told me she thought I should slow things down. She wanted to make sure I was fully over Sylvie before I hurried into marriage with Robin.

At the time, I was stubbornly certain that Robin was what I needed. Robin made me feel less raw inside. She calmed me. She was my shot at redemption. And in the end, yes. She was what I needed. But it's clear to me now that marrying someone because they're everything you need at the time isn't love. It's the worst kind of selfishness.

It's been six months since Robin's murder. For the past several days, I've been sitting in the courthouse at Brian Raymond's trial, and this afternoon, the jury found him guilty.

I see his guilt. I'm relieved that the jury got it right and that he'll face punishment for what he did.

But I see my own guilt, too.

I wasn't over Sylvie when I married Robin. I'm still not over Sylvie.

Occasionally, I still long for Sylvie so much that it feels like a fist squeezing my heart. I'm still so angry at her that my fingers curl into fists when I think about the day she left us. I still dream about her. I still have a hard time containing my hostility whenever she calls or sends Willow a letter or a present.

Every once in a while, I'll see a van like the one Sylvie drove off in and for a split second, I'll think that Sylvie's come home and joy will run through me before I catch myself. Joy? Over Sylvie?

I'm still screwed up over her. I wish to God that it weren't true. Other than bringing Robin back to life, I want nothing more than to be done with Sylvie. I've been trying to get over her—to *be* over her—for years now. I married someone else. I had another child. And still, I'm not over Sylvie.

That fact fills me with shame. I'm brutally ashamed because Robin's dead, and because she loved me, and because she gave me a beautiful daughter, and because she deserved my undivided love. But that's not what I gave her.

My only consolation is that I believe Robin felt loved by me. I did everything a good husband should do and more. She often told me how wonderful I was to her and the girls.

In the courtroom, I thought about how she used to tell me that while guilt ate and ate at me.

God, let Robin never have known that she didn't have my whole heart. And please, please forgive me.

I don't know how to move on from Sylvie. What I do know is that my history with Sylvie and Robin makes it clear that I'm not worthy of relationships. I never want to fall in love again. And I definitely don't want to marry again.

I'm an idiot with women.

I'm too selfish to be trusted.

Garner's Journal Entry

Brian Raymond hung himself in prison.

He took the coward's way out, but then, I shouldn't be surprised about that. His actions toward women proved him to be a coward a long time ago.

I can't work up any compassion for his family. Or any pleasure over his death. Or any forgiveness toward Brian. If Robin were here, she could probably find a way to forgive him. But he took her life and so there's only me.

All I feel in the face of Brian's suicide is grim acceptance.

Death is what he deserved. Death is what he got.

CHAPTER

Six

Phone Message from Margaret to Her Daughter, Kathleen

Dorothy just called and told me that she heard Dominic Bradford died of a heart attack. It's just terrible. So sudden. He was only sixty-five.

I feel for his wife, of course. Although, at least Dominic's wife, Elizabeth, has grandchildren to comfort her. Unlike me. So really, her life is practically wine and roses compared to mine. You don't know how I mourn the fact that I may never have grandchildren.

Anyhow. Dorothy said that Dominic's son, Garner, will almost certainly inherit Bradford Shipping. Little good that will do him, since the company is said to be on the verge of bankruptcy.

Garner's wife died just what? Two years ago? And now his father. Gone, too.

I expect that Garner will pay off Bradford Shipping's creditors and close the company's doors. In light of that, it seems to me that now's the time for you to leave Bradford Shipping. Don't you think so, Kathleen? You've proven yourself to be quite persistent, but look—the writing is on the wall.

Call me back right away, please.

Phone Conversation between Kathleen and Garner

GARNER: May I speak with Kathleen Burke, please?

KATHLEEN: Speaking.

GARNER: Ms. Burke, this is Garner Bradford.

KATHLEEN: Oh! Yes. Certainly, Mr. Bradford. It's nice to hear from you. What can I do for you?

GARNER: I was packing up my father's office and found eight reports in a box in his storage closet. The reports appear to be written by you. Is that correct?

KATHLEEN: Yes. Yes, that's correct. I wanted to say, sir, that I'm very sorry for your loss.

GARNER: Thank you.

KATHLEEN: You said that you found the reports in a closet in your father's office?

GARNER: Yes. Every one of these is an inch thick. Did my father assign you to write them as some sort of special project?

KATHLEEN: No, I took it upon myself to write them. Whenever I noticed an area of the company that offered room for, ah, improvement, I researched the subject and typed up a report.

GARNER: How many years have you been with the company?

KATHLEEN: Almost four and a half years.

GARNER: You've taken it upon yourself to write eight reports in four and a half years?

KATHLEEN: Right. It was always my hope that your father would find them useful.

GARNER: And did he?

KATHLEEN: I don't think so. He never contacted me to discuss them. Actually, this is the first confirmation I've had that he even received them. I have no way of knowing whether he read them or not.

GARNER: Ah.

KATHLEEN: Do *you* happen to know if he read them?

GARNER: I'm afraid I don't. Have we met?

KATHLEEN: No. I've attended a few of the company picnics that you've attended, but I haven't had an opportunity to introduce myself.

GARNER: Well, your eight reports have done a pretty good job of introducing you, Ms. Burke.

KATHLEEN: It seems they have.

GARNER: Once I've had a chance to look over them, my secretary will call you to schedule a meeting. All right?

KATHLEEN: Yes! That . . . that sounds great.

GARNER: Good. Oh, and Kathleen?

KATHLEEN: Yes?

GARNER: Ease back on the report writing at least until I can get through these, okay?

KATHLEEN: Aye aye.

Phone Message from Kathleen to Her Friend Rose

Oh my gosh, Rose, I know you're at work and can't answer. Even so, I had to tell you that Garner Bradford himself just called me. He found the reports I wrote and he said he's going to look over them!

I was a little flustered and excited and so I ended our conversation by saying aye aye.

Aye aye? Why did I say that? It's so weird that I said that.

I'm regretting the aye aye and I'm regretting the fact that I didn't have the reports professionally edited. What if there are typos in them? If there are, he might think I'm sloppy at punctuation when you and I both know I'm excellent at punctuation. A real stickler.

If he loves my reports, it could mean a promotion.

But ahhhh! What if he hates my reports? That

could mean a demotion.

How long do you think it will take him to get back to me? I don't think I can bear to wait.

I might need to start drinking Alka-Seltzer.

Unsent Letter from Kathleen to Garner

Dear Garner,

Ever since our meeting earlier today, my head has been full of all the things I want to say to you but can't. So I finally decided to write them all down. Maybe after this, I'll be able to eat and relax and watch TV like I'd planned to do this evening. It's eight o'clock at night! I'd like to watch TV if that's okay with you.

I hope you'll overlook the fact that I'm jotting all this down on a "My Deepest Condolences" greeting card. It's all I had. Stationery isn't my strong suit. Which you don't need to know and won't know, since this card is going straight into the lowest drawer of my bedside table. It can hang out with all my dad's postcards, pictures from sorority formals during college, and the love letters my ex-boyfriend Rob sent me. He wanted to marry me, fyi, but marriage isn't a goal of mine.

I digress. Here's what I want to say to you.

First, thank you for reading my reports. Thank you for inviting me to meet with you. Thank you for listening to me as if I had something worthwhile to say. Thank you for looking at me as if I was an equal instead of a less-than. Which, frankly, despite women's lib, is pretty rare at Bradford Shipping from men in business suits.

Second, I'm miffed at you for only seeing merit in five of my eight recommendations. When you insisted in that measured way of yours that the other three recommendations were too expensive, you really didn't give me a chance to list the one thousand ways in which my ideas, while expensive at the outset, will make Bradford Shipping money in the long run.

I'm still trying to decide whether you're being a knucklehead about those three reports or whether there's any slight, slim chance that you might be right about those three reports. I'm leaning toward knucklehead.

Third, you're not quite what I expected. Catching a few glimpses of you from a distance didn't prepare me for the force of you close up and in person.

You're taller than I'd guessed. How tall are you? 5'11"? You're not an extraordinarily tall man but something about your bearing or your posture or the fact that you now own the majority share of Bradford Shipping makes you seem tall. Even in my heels, I felt as though I had to look quite a ways up to meet your eyes.

You're both more weathered and more calm than I thought you'd be. You're only two years older than I am, but you seem ten years older. There's a steadiness about you that surprised me, that's very rare in men as young as you are. I suppose you were forced to develop that steadiness in order to survive the difficulties you've been through. The death of your wife, the death of your father, and the strain of inheriting a troubled company are heavy weights to carry. Are your shoulders strong enough to carry all that plus two little girls?

Your eyes are beautiful. Which is definitely something I'll never tell you in person. But they *are* beautiful. They're a mesmerizing shade of translucent jade green. Your eyes shook me a little bit, to tell the truth.

Fourth, I won't be staying long. I want to help you save Bradford Shipping. I do. I want that because this company is the largest employer in the area, because Bradford Shipping has a long and respectable history, because there's much about the company that's worth saving, and because playing an integral role in the company's turn-around would be great for me career-wise.

However, as soon as Estée Lauder comes through with a job offer, I'm gone. I expect to be wearing cute winter coats and eating bagels in New York City soon.

Respectfully,
Kathleen E. Burke

CHAPTER

Seven

Garner's Journal Entry

My father died.

He had his faults. He set extremely high expectations for Glenna and me. He was a harsh disciplinarian. I can't remember a time when he told me he loved me. But he had his strengths, also. He was a loyal husband to my mother. He worked hard. He wasn't afraid of responsibility.

All my life, my father was there, like a pillar holding up a house. And now, without warning, he's gone. He went like Robin did. There, then not.

My life feels strange without him in it.

The house is beginning to cave in without one of its central pillars.

I really don't know if Bradford Shipping can

avoid bankruptcy. For a long time now, I've been advocating for sweeping changes that would allow us to compete better in the marketplace. My father used to tell me the company couldn't afford those changes, and I used to think his answer was mostly motivated by stubbornness. Now that I have access to all the financials, I understand how little capital remains. If I overextend Bradford Shipping in order to pay for changes, there's a chance I could save the company. There's a bigger chance that I'll end up writing the company's death warrant.

The longtime employees of Bradford Shipping and the residents of this community have judged me to be too young and inexperienced to lead a business of this size. They expect me to fail. I'm sure the owners of West Coast Transporters are rubbing their hands together as they wait for the inevitable.

I want to do right by the employees who depend on Bradford Shipping to provide for their families. I also want to honor Frederick Bradford, who founded the company, and all the other Bradfords between him and me who poured their lives and their pride into this business.

Deep down, though, I'm overwhelmed. And weary.

I ran down the hallways of this company when

I was a kid. I grew up listening to my father talk about this company every night at the dinner table. I started working here in the summers when I was sixteen. I've had a full-time position here since I graduated from college.

I'm only twenty-eight. I only inherited Bradford Shipping two weeks ago. Yet already, I'm weary.

Most of the time, I inwardly agree with the employees and the community about the likelihood of my failure. I am the wrong man for this job. I don't have the strength or the skill or the energy to rescue this century-old company.

Nonetheless, I'm the boss. My father died and I inherited Bradford Shipping. So if anyone is going to rescue this company, it's going to have to be me.

Garner's Journal Entry

I have an employee named Kathleen.

Even though she looks like a beach girl who should be selling ice cream at the shore, she's desperate to be taken seriously. She tries hard to come across as mature and polished. Instead she comes across as sheltered, green, and idealistic.

Kathleen is full of determination and enthusiasm.

Kathleen makes me feel old and cynical.

The company doesn't need old and cynical. It needs determination and enthusiasm and people like Kathleen who can bring new ideas to the table.

I created a task force. It includes Kathleen, who represents the Customer Service Department. Two financial analysts. One manager. One HR person. One operations specialist. I've asked them to study every branch of the company. They'll evaluate strengths and weaknesses, conduct market research, and form strategies for the future.

I moved the task force members into offices on my floor of the admin building after forcing early retirement on several vice-presidents who'd been leeching off Bradford Shipping for decades. They were all my father's yes-men. None were open to change.

At this point it's change or die.

Phone Conversation between Garner and His Mother, Elizabeth

GARNER: One of the women who works for me mentioned that her mother had met you.

ELIZABETH: Oh? What's her mother's name?

GARNER: I'm not sure. My employee's name is Kathleen Burke. I'm guessing her mom would have the same last name since Kathleen's not married. I think she said she grew up around Snoqualmie.

ELIZABETH: The Burkes that I know of in that area own Atlas Aeronautics. They're all of Irish descent. Martin Burke started Atlas and he has to be, oh, close to eighty now. He's a wonderful man. Generous and smart. Much of Atlas's tremendous success is attributed to him.

GARNER: Do you know anything about Martin's family?

ELIZABETH: Now that Martin's getting up in years, I've heard that he's been giving his grandson, Shane Burke, more and more control. If Kathleen is Shane's sister, then their mother would be . . . let me think for a second. Margaret. Margaret Burke who, yes, I've met and spoken with. And that would mean that Kathleen's father was Martin's son, Dillon Burke.

GARNER: Was?

ELIZABETH: Dillon died a long time ago. Probably twenty years ago now.

GARNER: How did he die?

ELIZABETH: Flying one of the company's planes. There was a crash. . . . It was a terrible tragedy. I know that Martin took Dillon's family under his wing after the accident. He's provided for Margaret very comfortably ever since.

GARNER: Interesting.

ELIZABETH: If the Kathleen Burke who works for you is Margaret and Dillon's daughter, I wonder why she's not working for Atlas Aeronautics.

GARNER: She's about as independent as they come.

ELIZABETH: Is she . . . ? Are you . . . interested in going out with her?

GARNER: No. Not at all. Just curious.

CHAPTER

Eight

Phone Message from Margaret to Her Daughter, Kathleen

Hello? Kathleen? Goodness, still not answering your phone? Are you doing nothing but working these days? That's not good for your complexion, you know. You'll develop bags under your eyes.

Shane just told me that you've moved into an office near Garner Bradford himself. Kathleen Evangeline! Isn't it as clear as clear can be that God is punishing that man for the child he had out of wedlock? Judgment is sure to follow him wherever he goes.

Phone Conversation between Kathleen and Her Friend Rose

KATHLEEN: You're not in labor yet, are you?

ROSE: No, unfortunately. I've been eating spicy food and walking a lot more than a person the size of a whale should ever walk and I still can't get this baby to budge.

KATHLEEN: Do you have time to talk me down about my mother?

ROSE: The usual?

KATHLEEN: The usual.

Phone Conversation between Kathleen and Her Friend Rose

KATHLEEN: Does baby Jenny love the outfit I sent?

ROSE: Yes, indeed. She keeps going on and on about it.

KATHLEEN: I miss her already. Tell her not to grow too much between now and when I drive up for a visit next weekend.

ROSE: You sure sound happy for someone who's missing my baby.

KATHLEEN: My new office makes me happy. I have windows! I have room for potted plants!

ROSE: From taking complaints over a headset to an office on the same floor as the owner of the company in just four years. That must be some kind of record.

KATHLEEN: *Just* four years? The past four years have felt to me like fourteen.

Unsent Letter from Kathleen to Garner

Garner,

You, sir, are unfailingly gentlemanly.

I spend time on my hair and makeup each morning. I wear flattering clothing and excellent shoes. I even bought a fantastic new pair of earrings. Yet, never once in the month that I've been working with the task force, have you looked at me with anything other than completely professional courtesy.

When are you planning on looking at me with something other than completely professional courtesy?

Never?

Never is fine with me, of course. I have no plans to date my boss. I'm far too career-minded for that. Also, I should tell you that I prefer boyfriends who don't have French ex-girlfriends, who haven't been married previously, and who don't have children.

You're not ideal.

So it's fine that you don't find me attractive. Really. It's better this way.

Respectfully,
Kathleen E. Burke

p.s. By the way, it's idiotic of you to reject my proposal for new computer software. Your "It's too expensive, Kathleen" mantra makes me want to scream.

p.s.s. In every other way, you're lovely to work with. You're thoughtful and principled and decent. So please don't take the idiotic comment above too personally.

CHAPTER

Nine

Garner's Journal Entry

I've developed a habit. Every night when I leave for home, I glance down the hallway as I'm walking to the elevators to see whether the light is on in Kathleen's office. It always is. She stays later than I do *every day*.

And why shouldn't she? She's not a single parent, so she has the freedom to work long hours.

I have no idea why that light in her office both irritates me and comforts me.

I can't decide if I should give her a raise, or tell her to get a life, or talk her into taking self-defense classes.

What I do know: I'm tempted every night to tell her how dangerous the world is for women who walk through parks or parking lots alone.

What happened to Robin has made me unreasonably afraid, I know that. I worry all the time about Willow and Nora and the women in my life. I never leave my girls with anyone except Valentina or family members. Glenna and my mom have grown tired of my overprotectiveness.

So far, I've managed to bite my tongue each night as I'm leaving the office. It's not my place to lecture Kathleen. She's a grown woman who can take care of herself. She's a co-worker, nothing more. I'm aware that if I do break down and say something to her one of these nights, she's more likely to think I'm crazy than to thank me for my concern.

Garner's Journal Entry

I'm having a hard time concentrating at work.

Why in the world did I give the task force members offices on my floor? It seemed like a good idea at the time . . . to evict the old guard and move in the staff that represented the company's one hope for the future. I regret it now, though, because I can't go an hour without seeing Kathleen Burke.

I can't remember when I've felt this frustrated, and that's saying a lot because I have two preschoolers at home.

I noticed Kathleen's attractiveness the day we met. I noticed it the same way that I might notice that a woman's hair is gray. It was just a fact. It didn't matter to me or affect me.

A month and a half has passed since then.

A month and a half of me sitting in the board room during task force meetings, watching Kathleen give presentations on newfound information she feels passionately about. She always feels passionately about the information she presents.

A month and a half of looking up from my desk and seeing her slender body pass by my office in tailored skirts and silky shirts.

A month and a half of disagreeing with her over new computer software. When she thinks I'm being pig-headed, her nose scrunches and her brown eyes blaze. My mom told me that her family is Irish. It's obviously true. Kathleen has the fiery will and the red glint in her hair to prove it. She can't seem to understand that I'm not being pig-headed about new computer software. I'm just being right.

A month and a half of running into her in the

break room. She tilts her head when she refills her coffee mug, which causes her long hair to slide over her shoulder and upper arm.

A month and a half of hearing her laughter from a distance.

A month and a half of receiving correspondence from her signed "Respectfully, Kathleen E. Burke." Why the E? There are no Kathleen R. or B. or K. Burkes who work at Bradford Shipping. The E is pretentious.

A month and a half of looking back every evening when I leave and seeing her office light on.

Kathleen's attractiveness is more than a fact to me now. She's annoyingly pretty, she's persistent, and she's impossible to ignore.

For more than two years, I've been loyal to Robin's memory. That's how I want things to continue. That's how I like it.

Willow and Nora are my life. I spend every hour outside of work with them, and I'm exhausted at the end of each day. There's no room in my schedule or in my emotions for a relationship. I'm even more certain that I'm not meant to be a boyfriend or a husband now than I was when Robin died. So the distraction of Kathleen makes me feel like I'm betraying a commitment I made to myself. Which, in turn, makes me angry.

I've been asking God to take away this stupid pull I feel toward Kathleen. Or better yet, to give her a new job in another city or state.

My goals since Robin died are simple: Focus on my girls when I'm at home. Concentrate on my responsibilities when I'm at work.

That's all. Two goals.

I want peace. I want to live the life that's before me—alone.

CHAPTER
Ten

Unsent Letter from Kathleen to Garner

Dear Garner,

My mom keeps warning me to stay away from you. She doesn't seem to comprehend that her warnings are making you more and more attractive to me. As I mentioned in my last letter, dating you was never in my plans!

Well, you do have those eyes. It's not possible to be totally uninterested in a man with eyes like yours. But I was doing my best. Ninety percent of me didn't plan to date you.

But now my mother has stepped in numerous times to insist I can't have you, and my rebellious heart, which has always pined for what she forbids, is beginning to find you more than a little bit tempting.

I like the way you roll your collared shirts up at the cuffs, for example.

I like the sporty, bracing scent of your soap.

I like how purely focused you are on business.

I like the finger tracks in your dark hair.

I like the sorrow lines beside your eyes and lips.

I like that you keep the temperature in your office at sixty-six degrees. Entering your office is like walking into the beginning of winter. Invigorating.

I like how, when we have task force lunches, you never eat green vegetables. You'll eat orange, red, and yellow veggies, but you have taken an amusingly firm stance against green.

And I like your rare smiles so much that I catch my breath each time I spot one.

If my mom keeps this up, I can't be responsible for my actions.

Except I will be. Responsible for my actions. I always am. Don't worry, Garner. I've read what the experts say about girls who lose their fathers. How, when they grow up, they look for men to supply the love they never received from their dad. I know all about that, so you can bet I won't be making that mistake. No, sirree. Rest easy.

Bagels and corporate glory are (and will always be) calling me east.

Respectfully,
Kathleen

Unsent Letter from Kathleen to Garner

Garner,

Here's something you should know about me. I've had boyfriends over the years, but I've never taken any of them seriously because I don't want to settle down. I'm not the domestic type. My mother was and is the domestic type and I want this apple of mine to fall very, very far from her tree.

Marriage didn't work out that well for my mom. She'd tell you differently because she loved my dad. She loved him so much that when he died, she was wrecked. She lost not only her husband, but a big part of her job because her job was to care for him and for us. She responded to his death by grieving and suffocating her kids. Suffocating her kids and grieving. In ways that are hard to explain, my dad's death ended up hardening sections of my mom's heart.

I want to accomplish things completely separate from family. I want to travel and have adventures and see the world. I don't want to need people as much as my mom needs my brother and me. I don't want to base my life on a man who can die or divorce me.

You know all about losing people, Garner. So I'm certain you can understand my reluctance to depend too much on others.

I simply cannot fall for you.

Kathleen

Phone Conversation between Kathleen and Her Friend Rose

KATHLEEN: I think I'm falling for Garner Bradford.

ROSE: What! Hang on a minute. Let me pass the baby to Henry so I can concentrate on this conversation. One sec. Okay. I'm in my bedroom with the door closed. You're falling for Garner Bradford?

KATHLEEN: I've been trying hard not to and I've been doing an okay job of it, but the company held one of its family barbecue picnics this afternoon. I went and he was there with his girls and it melted me. Seeing him with them.

ROSE: More details, please.

KATHLEEN: I was talking with one of the women from accounting when I spotted him getting into the food line with the girls. I excused myself and hurried over because it looked like he could use an extra hand. He can't very well hold three plates at once, right?

ROSE: Right.

KATHLEEN: I ended up filling his daughter Willow's plate.

ROSE: Which one is Willow?

KATHLEEN: The older one. She's four. Nora, the younger one, is two. After I carried Willow's plate to their table, Garner was sort of honor-bound to invite me to join them. So I sat down, and when I looked across the table, I saw that Garner had a burger exactly like mine. We both chose the bun with sesame seeds. We both put tomatoes and pickles and grilled onions and ketchup and mustard on ours.

ROSE: Let me guess. Neither one of your burgers

had lettuce.

KATHLEEN: Exactly! No lettuce.

ROSE: It sounds like fate.

KATHLEEN: That's what I thought. It felt more and more like fate the longer I sat there. Willow is serious and quiet. Nora is sweet and busy. They're gorgeous little girls, Rose.

ROSE: I'm sure they are.

KATHLEEN: And Garner was wonderful with them. He used a wet wipe to clean their hands. He cut their hot dogs into tiny pieces. He brought their sippy cups out of his bag. He redid Willow's ponytail when it started to sag. The girls look at him like he hung the moon.

ROSE: And by the time you finished your lettuce-free hamburger, you were looking at him like he hung the moon, too.

KATHLEEN: Yes.

ROSE: Mm-hmm.

KATHLEEN: The girls finished before we did. He unhooked balloons from the center of our table and tied them around their wrists. They ran around on the grass next to the table with their balloons while we finished. I told him how great they were. He asked me what I was like when I was little and I found myself telling him, Rose. About how my knees were always scraped and my shoes were always scuffed. About how I believed that if I practiced hard enough, I could be better than the boys at soccer. About how I agreed to let my mom dress me in a ruffly dress and take me to a cotillion so that in return she'd take me to the stable for horseback riding lessons.

ROSE: And how did he respond?

KATHLEEN: He listened and asked questions and seemed to understand. We talked about his childhood in Merryweather. Then about what it's like to lose a dad, since we've both been through that.

ROSE: Wow.

KATHLEEN: Falling for him is not in my plan, Rose!

ROSE: Maybe it's not in your plan, but does it have to be a bad thing?

KATHLEEN: It's a terrible thing.

ROSE: Why?

KATHLEEN: He's not interested in me, for starters. Also, he's my boss. Also, my job at Bradford Shipping is just a consolation prize until Estée Lauder comes through. I'm not staying in Washington. You know I'm not.

ROSE: Okay, so since this crush of yours isn't going anywhere, there's no need to panic.

KATHLEEN: All of a sudden, though, I really wish it *was* going somewhere.

ROSE: It can't until he decides he's interested in you, too. My advice is to go on doing what you've been doing—working hard and being professional. Be patient. Good things come . . .

KATHLEEN: . . . to those who wait.

Unsent Letter from Kathleen to Garner

Garner,

It's been a week since the picnic. It's as if our

conversation that day gave me a ticket, a ticket that now allows me to talk with you about things other than Bradford Shipping and the task force.

We chatted about Nora's love of board books in the break room over coffee. I joked about my mother in the hallway. You told me about your sister when we were the first two to arrive in the conference room.

It's been delightful. I only wish I could be fully content with the ticket I've been given. I do value it. A lot. I realize that it's probably a very rare ticket.

Yet instead of being fully content with it, I find myself looking at you and wondering what you'd do if I ran a fingertip down your wrist. Or kissed the side of your neck. Or ruffled your hair.

You are a very controlled man. I admire that about you. At the same time, I'm becoming almost desperate to test your control.

What happened to the reckless young man you once were? The one who had a tempestuous love affair with a French artist named Sylvie Rolland? (Yes, I've done my research. Sue me.)

What happened to the man who was so given to emotion or attraction or destiny or whatever that he walked down the aisle to marry Robin Bowman just twelve months after Sylvie left?

I suspect that Robin's death hammered the spontaneity and what was left of your youth out of you. I wonder if there's still passion in you, though. Deep emotion. Love?

I want to know. I want to be the one to stir those things in you. I want to see if your reserve can crack. I want to kiss you.

I won't.

But I want to. It's the worst thing in the world to like someone who doesn't like you in return. But it's the best thing, too. It's a sweet, hot, tingly, aching, delicious pain.

Phone Message from Kathleen to Her Friend Rose

Where are you? I need you to answer. Of all the times for you not to answer, this is the worst.

I just kissed Garner.

Oh my gosh. Rose! What am I going to do?

Today was a long, hard, long—did I already say long?—day. I was working here at my desk and I was incredibly frustrated because I was having to fix a mistake one of the financial analysts made, when I heard a knock. I looked up and Garner was standing just inside my doorway, with his suit jacket over his arm. My heart squeezed because . . . you know why. This thing I have for him.

He asked me why I always work so late. I explained about the mistake I was fixing and then told him about all the other things I still have to finish before I can call it a night.

He said he thought it was dangerous for me to remain on our floor after hours, to walk to my car alone, to arrive at my apartment alone. He told me he was concerned that I'm being careless with my safety.

I stared at him, speechless, because lots of people work late. Almost all of them are men, so the only thing I could figure was that he was basically scolding me for working late because I'm female. Which is completely sexist and infuriating. But hold the phone. It gets worse.

"Going home earlier will be better for you in other ways," he said. "It'll help you balance things out. Get more sleep. More rest." And then this is the kicker. He said, "It might be time for you to get a life, Kathleen."

He said it nicely. There was humor in his eyes, there was. But I knew . . . *I knew*, Rose, that he was serious. That he really does think I need to get a life.

And it just . . . it sparked something inside me

because here I am working my butt off for Bradford Shipping, spending my time at the office, because I'm trying to *save his company*. He's the one leaving to go home and he has the audacity to tell me to get a life!

I stood and came around my desk as I told him all of that. Everything I just told you. I didn't scream it. I spoke it quickly and I think, quietly. But I said it like I meant it. Because I did mean it. I was upset.

How dare he! Get a life! From the man who's not exactly known for making the best life decisions. I found myself standing right in front of him.

He raised an eyebrow slightly. That's it! That's all he did.

He was totally unmoved by my speech. He looked calm. He looked like someone I could never have. Plus, his eyes are ridiculous.

My destructive streak surfaced and I stepped forward and I put my palms on his cheeks and I kissed him. Just a press of lips to lips. That's it. I waited for maybe one whole second, which felt like ten, for him to kiss me back, to put his arms around me. Something! Instead he moved backward.

Oh, Rose. It was horrible.

His gaze narrowed on me and his chest expanded with his breath a few times, but otherwise he stood there like a statue. And I stood there like a statue. Then he turned and left.

I could die. I've locked my office door and closed my blinds and I'm sitting on the floor behind my desk. How am I supposed to face him now? I'm sure he thinks I'm insane.

Why did I kiss him? I can't believe I did that. I kissed him, Rose! He's my boss. And he doesn't like me. And I kissed him.

I'm in deep, deep trouble.

Handwritten Note Left on Garner's Desk

Dear Garner,

I'm sorry for my actions last night. I can't explain or justify what I did. There's no excuse for my behavior. It was unprofessional, and I deeply regret it.

I hope that you'll be able to forgive me and that we can proceed forward with our working relationship and friendship.

I apologize.

Respectfully,
Kathleen E. Burke

Typed Letter on Bradford Shipping Letterhead Left on Kathleen's Desk

Kathleen,

I accept your apology. I value your work ethic and the contributions you've made to Bradford Shipping. This company is facing a great many challenges. I think we can both agree that it would be wise to focus all our attention and efforts on meeting those challenges.

Sincerely,
Garner

CHAPTER
Eleven

Garner's Journal Entry

Kathleen kissed me.

I know she thinks I'm stuffy. That I didn't like the kiss. That I was offended by it.

I'm going to let her think those things because I wish they were true and because they've created a wall between us and I need a wall. What's true—what she doesn't know—is that she set off a thunderstorm of need inside me.

God, I don't understand you. I've prayed and prayed for you to take her or these feelings for her away. But you haven't.

Why?

Why are you allowing me to feel this way for Kathleen?

Garner's Journal Entry

Two weeks have passed since Kathleen kissed me. It's been tense and awkward between us. We don't talk unless it's necessary for work purposes.

I'm still praying. But instead of going away, the chemistry between us is only intensifying.

God, don't you hear me?

Please. I only want to live my life in peace.

CHAPTER

Twelve

Letter from Kathleen to Estée Lauder, Inc.

Dear Ms. Jenkins,

It is with great anticipation that I'm applying for the position of Account Representative in Estée Lauder, Inc.'s Customer Service Department. I've studied the job description, and I believe that I have the skills required.

Since graduating from Gonzaga University, I've accrued four and a half years of work experience at Bradford Shipping, America's premier Pacific shipping company.

It is my hope that after reviewing the newly updated résumé I've included, that you'll agree that I am the experienced, hard-working, and reliable employee you're looking for.

I'm grateful for the correspondence we've shared over the years, Ms. Jenkins. I'm looking forward to discussing the possibility of an interview with you, during which I'd be glad to further elaborate on how my abilities might benefit your organization. Thank you for your consideration. I look forward to your call.

Respectfully,
Kathleen E. Burke

Letter from Estée Lauder, Inc. to Kathleen

Dear Ms. Burke,

Thank you for contacting me. I'm sorry, but I filled the position of Account Representative just last week. I appreciate your continued interest in securing a job with Estée Lauder, and I admire your persistence.

I will certainly keep you in mind should other roles within the Customer Service Department become open.

Sincerely,
Susan Jenkins

Unsent Letter from Kathleen to Garner

Garner,

Do good things really come to those who wait? Or is that saying just a bunch of baloney someone made up so that inactive people could feel better about themselves? It seems to me that good things are far more likely to come to those who bulldoze ahead and make things happen.

I've been alternately waiting and trying to bulldoze my way into a job in New York for a long time. So far, no good thing has come my way on that front.

I can't figure out why God placed this dream in my heart if He plans to let it go unfulfilled.

Since I'll be staying at Bradford Shipping for the foreseeable future, I'm going to have to fix things between you and me, Garner, because I can't stand to feel this rigid and embarrassed every time our paths cross.

It's been three weeks since I kissed you. Three weeks may not be a long enough penance for an uninvited kiss. Nevertheless, I'm pronouncing it sufficient because this awful strain between us cannot continue.

It just can't, Garner. Okay?

CHAPTER
Thirteen

Garner's Journal Entry

I was finishing lunch at Orton's today when Kathleen came in. The minute I saw her, I started gathering up the papers I'd been reading, in preparation to leave. Before I had them in a stack, she sat down across from me at my table.

I didn't know what to say, so I said, "How can I help you?"

I sounded and probably looked like an uptight old man. But again, my exterior and interior were nothing alike. I was rattled. By her direct eye contact and by her beauty and by her silky shirt. I've had it with her silky shirts. Today's shirt was ice blue.

"Listen," she said. "Things have been uncomfortable between us lately. It's all my fault and I'm really, really sorry. I'd like it if we could talk like two normal people from now on. Can I bribe you into that by buying you dessert?" And then she smiled. Her smile was full of self-deprecation and persuasiveness.

I told her there was no need to bribe me, that talking to her like a normal person sounded fine to me.

"I demand a chance to bribe you," she said. "What's your favorite dessert?"

I told her it was chocolate cake. Then I tried to convince her that she didn't need to buy me chocolate cake, but she was already out of her chair and hurrying to the counter. She came back with a to-go box. She said she'd gotten the cake to go because she could see I was headed back to the office and didn't want to keep me. "Maybe this'll be just the thing when midafternoon exhaustion hits you," she said. Then she smiled again.

Clearly, I remember every word she said.

I found myself smiling back at her over the box of cake. In fact, I smiled all the way back to Bradford Shipping, a two-block walk.

The cake was delicious.

Garner's Journal Entry

It's been a month since I've written, since Kathleen bribed me with chocolate cake. Her bribe worked.

She was real and honest with me at Orton's, which has allowed me to let my guard down slightly with her. Since that day at Orton's, we've gotten along well. We're friends. And everything would be fine if my feelings for her were only friendly. Instead attraction rushes to life, powerful and insistent, every single time we're together. I can't ignore it. I can't move past it.

Kathleen makes me laugh. She frustrates me. She pushes me to defend the business decisions I make.

I want to be more to her than her friend. Here's why that can't happen:

1) I can't keep Kathleen safe. I'm not interested in adding a woman to my life and to my girls' lives who could be taken from us violently. The girls and I could not survive that again.

2) Kathleen's driven and determined and ambitious, exactly like my father was. Work is the thing that she cares about most. I know from experience that it's rough to

care about someone who cares more about their job than they do about you.

3) She's independent, exactly like Sylvie. Again, I know from experience that it's no good to care about someone who's willing to leave you behind to chase their own dreams.

I've just read back over the above. The last two comparisons I made aren't completely fair to Kathleen. She's much kinder than my father was. She's much less selfish than Sylvie was.

I'm still praying that God will take away my feelings for Kathleen. But I'm no longer praying that He'll take Kathleen away.

I couldn't stand it if she left.

Garner's Journal Entry

My mom insisted that Willow and Nora and I move into Bradfordwood. Since I was a kid, I've known that I'd one day live at Bradfordwood and one day become the CEO of Bradford Shipping. I just never expected either of those things to happen so soon.

Glenna and I tried to convince Mom to stay at

Bradfordwood, but she was determined to move into a place less filled with memories of Dad, a smaller place. Bradfordwood sits on two hundred acres. Almost every foot of the house's ten thousand square feet needs renovation that we can't afford at this point. The responsibility of all of that was no longer something my mom wanted to deal with, so she's now in a brand-new row house in Merryweather and the girls and I are here, at Bradfordwood.

Whenever Willow and Nora have stayed here over the years, they've slept in the pink guest bedroom. That's where they're still sleeping, even though there are seven bedrooms and I told them they could each take their pick. I think they're a little scared of this big, old-fashioned brick house.

Willow asked, now that we've moved into Grandma's house, if Mommy's going to come back to live with us. Even though I could see resignation in her face when she asked the question, I could also see hope. She understood that it was probably impossible. Even so, my little realist was wishing against all odds that Robin would return.

I had to tell her that no, Mommy isn't coming back. I assured her that she could count on me, that I wasn't going anywhere, and that I loved her.

I'm often aware, though, that I'm just as susceptible to death as Robin. What if something happens to me? An accident or a terminal illness?

Should God let me live a long life, and I hope He does for Willow and Nora's sake, then I'll spend it taking care of them. My future is mapped out.

I'm not a man who's free. My birthright and my past decisions have made sure of that. Willow, Nora, Glenna, my mom, and the people at Bradford Shipping are depending on me and so I try hard not to let selfish desires worm their way into my life.

But I have come to want one selfish thing, despite all my best efforts.

I want Kathleen. It's been two months since she bribed me with chocolate cake.

I think about her all the time. At work. At home.

My track record with women is terrible. Loving her would probably doom either her or me. But still, I want her.

Note from Sylvie Left in Her Neighbor's Mailbox

Cherie,

I've decided to take a spontaneous holiday to America! I miss tacos, and the green mountains of Washington, and American men. I should be gone for no more than a week and a half. Will you be so kind as to collect my mail and water my flowers while I'm away?

I'm looking forward to seeing my daughter and her handsome papa.

I'll bring a bag of Tootsie Rolls back for you!

XO XO, Sylvie

CHAPTER
Fourteen

Unsent Letter from Kathleen to Garner

I'm in love with you.

I am.

This is totally new for me, Garner. With the boyfriends I've had in the past, we started with attraction and then moved on to dating and then stalled out there, long before love ever hit.

With you, we started with a business relationship that got tangled up with attraction and then moved on to friendship and now, here I am, in love with you. I'm amazed that I can love someone I'm not dating and haven't even kissed (except once).

I love how you are with your daughters. I love your sad, solitary heart. I love your patience and your intelligence and your goodness.

You've certainly never told me that you care for me. But often, I think I can see how you feel about me in your eyes, and then I'm filled with crazy, probably foolish, hope.

I'm not going to be the one to make a move, Garner. No how. No way. I already made the first move and it turned into a debacle.

So, please. Make a move on me. At your earliest convenience.

Letter from Kathleen to Her Father, Dillon

Daddy,

I'm desperate to share this with someone, but it feels too new and private even to share with Rose at the moment, so I'm going to tell you because I know you'll keep this just between us, same as when I broke Mom's lamp when I was six. Remember? You hugged me and dried my tears and said you'd tell her you bumped it over. Then you cleaned up the mess. As you carried the last of the broken pieces to the trash, you winked at me and said we'd keep this just between us.

It's a Monday, which means I hadn't seen Garner since Friday. I'm always the first one to arrive at work on Monday mornings because I'm so eager to see him again after the weekend. I waited and waited for him to arrive, but he didn't. Finally, someone mentioned he was out of the office on business. I felt like a kid who'd arrived at Disneyland only to be told the park was closed for the day.

As I was leaving work this evening, riding down in the elevator alone and depressed, the doors opened on the floor below mine. And there he was. Garner. He grinned at me and stepped into the elevator. The doors slid closed.

"Did I finally stay at work as late as you?" he asked.

I mumbled in the affirmative. It's hard to be witty when happiness is shooting through you like rockets.

"Staying as late as you is a first," he said.

"I'm trying to get a life," I told him. Inside joke. Which I suddenly worried wasn't very funny. But, thank you Lord, he chuckled and we kept staring at each other. Still smiling.

Then the humor began to fade from his face.

And then! Then he kissed me.

I barely had time to adjust, to kiss him back, before the elevator binged to signal that we'd reached the lobby.

We stepped apart quickly and walked side by side through the first floor of Bradford Shipping without glancing at each other once. I mostly looked down because I didn't want anyone, including him, to see my blush, which felt about as hot as the Arabian Peninsula. I was both thrilled and terrified that he'd find a reason to regret the kiss.

When we reached the parking lot, we faced each other. March wind that smelled like the start of spring raked through my hair. Light rain fell over us, softer than down, quieter than air.

I had to bite my lip to keep from saying something completely ill-advised such as, "I love you!" or "Please, please don't hurt me." Hope built within me painfully while I waited for him to speak.

"Should I leave a note of apology on your desk tomorrow morning?" he asked. He was teasing, but there was also a flicker of uncertainty in his expression. I realized that he was worried that he'd overstepped.

"No," I told him. "I hope you plan to repeat what just happened many more times. I'll only require a note of apology if you plan to stop. Not if you plan to continue."

Relief softened his jaw. "I plan to continue."

"Good," I said.

"Good," he said.

Then we nodded and walked in separate directions to our cars.

He finally made a move!!!!

If you could see me, you'd see that my hands are shaking a little and that I'm alight with joy. I'm a career girl who doesn't fall for men!

At least, that's who I used to be.

I didn't know until now what a powerful force love is. It was easy to scoff at people who married, who built their life around their family . . . until now. Until him.

Now everything I thought I knew and thought I wanted is changing beneath my feet like earth furrowed by an earthquake.

I love you so much, Daddy.

I miss you.

Thank you for keeping this just between us.

Kathleen

p.s. I had so much to tell you that I hope you'll understand why I didn't write on a postcard, as per our usual tradition.

CHAPTER

Fifteen

Garner's Journal Entry

I resisted Kathleen for as long as I could. For months I've been bolting down my tenderness for her. Forcing my muscles not to move or act in response to it.

I don't even know if she realizes that her gaze dropped to my lips in the elevator this evening. But when it did, that was it. Heat flashed through me and no bolt was strong enough to stop me.

I kissed her and I'm not sorry. But I am worried.

My reasons for avoiding relationships since Robin's death are right. They're valid. It's with deep reservations that I set those reasons to the side to make just enough room for something that matters to me even more.

Kathleen.

Is there a chance that things might end well for us? A lot of people have long, happy relationships. My parents, my grandparents on both sides, aunts and uncles, friends.

Neither of my past relationships took me to a destination I wanted so it's difficult for me to think that this one could. But there *has* to be a chance that Kathleen will stay safe and healthy. That I'll be able to add her into my life and my girls' lives without doing damage to us all. That things between Kathleen and I might work out.

There has to be a chance. Right?

Phone Conversation between Kathleen and Garner

KATHLEEN: How long have we been talking?

GARNER: An hour and . . . forty-five minutes. It's late. We should probably hang up so we can get some sleep.

KATHLEEN: Probably.

GARNER: I don't want to say good night.

KATHLEEN: Me neither. Let's talk for five more minutes.

Handwritten Note Left on Kathleen's Desk

May I take you to dinner some night soon? I'm willing to bribe you into going out with me with your favorite dessert, if necessary.

—Garner

Handwritten Note Left on Garner's Desk

Yes to dinner. Let me know what works with your family's schedule and we'll go then.

My favorite dessert is a hot fudge sundae with chopped peanuts. Put that in your back pocket and save for future reference.

—Kathleen

CHAPTER
Sixteen

Phone Message from Margaret to Her Daughter, Kathleen

Darling, Dorothy said she heard that Garner Bradford has a new girlfriend. I'm so glad that he's found someone. Now you and I don't have to worry about him settling his unwanted attentions on you.

I've never trusted men with light eyes.

Call me and we'll schedule brunch at the country club.

Phone Conversation between Kathleen and Garner

KATHLEEN: . . . so, you see, a job with Estée

Lauder has always been my big dream.

GARNER: I'm surprised they haven't hired you.

KATHLEEN: Thank you for saying that.

GARNER: Why do you think that working for that particular company has always been your big dream?

KATHLEEN: When I did that book report on Estée Lauder that I told you about, her story just . . . captured me.

GARNER: Why, though?

KATHLEEN: I'm not sure. Does it matter?

GARNER: It matters to me.

KATHLEEN: It does?

GARNER: I want to understand you. So quit stalling and answer my question. What was it about Estée Lauder that captured you?

KATHLEEN: The fact that she was both female and a hugely successful business person.

GARNER: And?

KATHLEEN: And I was a girl with a very overprotective mother. I was desperate for freedom. It seemed to me that if I could be like Estée, then I could be free.

GARNER: Ah.

KATHLEEN: I haven't thought this through quite this way before.

GARNER: It sounds to me like freedom is the thing you really want, Kathleen. That's your big dream. Do you think that's what's underneath your desire to work for Lauder?

KATHLEEN: Maybe.

GARNER: I have two kids and a company and an estate to take care of.

KATHLEEN: Yes.

GARNER: From my perspective, you *are* free.

KATHLEEN: I . . .

GARNER: Kathleen?

KATHLEEN: . . . I haven't ever felt free.

GARNER: Maybe it's time to start.

Unsent Letter from Kathleen to Garner

Garner,

We just got off the phone fifteen minutes ago after another of our long nightly phone conversations. I love our nightly phone conversations. I'm thankful to your girls for going to sleep at eight o'clock so that we can have them. I'm raising my mug of herbal tea to Willow and Nora!

It's one in the morning, yet I'm wide awake.

What you said to me earlier, about how, from your perspective, I'm free . . . it hit me like a freight train.

Goodness knows that God has had plenty of chances to give me a job at Estée Lauder if He'd wanted to. You told me once that you yourself prayed for quite some time that I'd find another job in another place. We were both praying for the same thing! But God said no to my prayers and yours.

It occurs to me, Garner, that I'm never going to get the position at Estée Lauder that I've wanted since the fourth grade.

Am I?

I'm sorry that I'm not. But I can see that you might be right. Perhaps I don't need a job at Estée

Lauder to achieve the thing I've always truly wanted most. It could be that my definition of success has been far too narrow. It could be that the time has come to set that old definition aside.

I'm an independent woman. I support myself. I contribute at the office. I'm no longer under my mother's control.

I'm free.

I've been striving so hard for so long, like a fish in a net, that I failed to stop and look around and realize I'm no longer trapped by the net. And haven't been for some time.

I'm free.

What's more, I'm content. That's been hard for me to say, to feel, in the past.

Actually, I'm more than content. I feel as though I'm one of the most fortunate women in the world because I'm crazy about you and you're crazy about me. (You're never going to see this so I can put words in your mouth.) Elation surges through me every time I make you smile. It's a small, elite, precious club to belong to—People Who Make Garner Happy. But by some miracle, I've become a part of it.

Love,
Kathleen

p.s. I'm still not tired.

p.s.s. I'm still content.

Phone Conversation between Kathleen and Her Friend Rose

ROSE: Take deep breaths and calm down and tell me what happened. Breathe. Breathe. Are you breathing?

KATHLEEN: I'm breathing.

ROSE: Now start over at the beginning. Slowly.

KATHLEEN: You knew that Garner invited me to his house for dinner tonight, didn't you?

ROSE: I did.

KATHLEEN: We've only been together for a week, but in that time, we've talked for hours every night. We've eaten lunch together every day at work. We've gone out to dinner once. And we've kissed, um, lots. The kisses have been . . .

ROSE: Amazing?

KATHLEEN: Yes. *He's* amazing. And it was a big deal that he invited me to his house to have dinner with his daughters. It's not like we were going to tell them that we're dating or anything like that, but still, it was a big deal. We were just starting to brown the meat to make sloppy joes and Willow was standing on a chair next to me because she wanted to help and everything was pretty much perfect, when the doorbell rang.

ROSE: And it was someone named Sylvie?

KATHLEEN: Yes. Sylvie is Willow's biological mother. When Garner led Sylvie into the kitchen, I just stood there frozen with a wooden spoon in my hand. Garner turned completely white and looked stricken. Not that Sylvie noticed. She swept Willow up and kissed her and then sat cross-legged on the floor and asked all of us enthusiastic questions. I answered for a while but the situation was just too weird. I could tell that I needed to leave so that Garner and the girls could deal with Sylvie's arrival. So that's what I did. And now they're probably eating sloppy joes. And I'm at home, having a heart attack.

ROSE: Huh. So this isn't the best turn of events.

KATHLEEN: No. Sylvie's incredibly beautiful, Rose. She's French and fabulous, and Garner's fabulous, too, and I'm scared that Sylvie will decide she wants him back.

ROSE: Even if she does, why would he take her back?

KATHLEEN: Because she was his first love. He's my first love, but she's his and first love is a *mighty force*. Plus, they have a child together.

ROSE: Garner's moved on from Sylvie.

KATHLEEN: I'm not sure that he has.

ROSE: Hasn't he?

KATHLEEN: I don't know. What I do know is that our relationship—mine and Garner's—is very, very new. If we were an established couple, I might feel differently. But as it is, I'm terrified that I'm going to lose him.

CHAPTER

Seventeen

Garner's Journal Entry

I just reread the first pages of this journal. I wrote them when Sylvie left, when I was desperate for her to come back. I loved Sylvie. I honestly did.

All these years later, I've gotten my wish. She came back.

She said she wanted to surprise us.

She surprised me all right. I felt the blood drain from my head when I opened the door and saw her there. She's just like I remember, but she's different, too. The whole time we ate dinner and talked, I struggled to get my head around the reality of her. Back in Washington. Inside our house.

The girls could tell things weren't right with me. They kept glancing at me doubtfully.

Willow and Nora were fascinated by Sylvie. They were also shy around her so they didn't say much, either. Sylvie kept the conversation going pretty much by herself.

After dinner, she brought out gifts for Willow and Nora. Toys and French caramels and clothes. The three of them had a great time playing. At one point, Willow mentioned to Sylvie that we have a hammock in the woods. Sylvie insisted on trying it, even though it was dark out and past the girls' bedtime. The three of us led Sylvie to the hammock. I stood there watching them swing wildly from side to side, roaring with laughter, until Nora threw up because she'd eaten too many caramels and Willow got motion sick and they both started crying.

After I got them bathed and in bed, I found Sylvie on the terrace, smoking a cigarette and drinking black coffee. She was sitting on a lounge chair and she looked like a still from a movie. Flawless.

She talked about Willow. She told me about her round-the-world tour and the life she made for herself in France when her tour ended. She asked me about my life. When we both fell silent, I could hear crickets and frogs. Stars hung above us. But the peaceful setting was in direct opposition to my emotions, which were dark and frustrated and angry.

She snuffed out her cigarette and set aside her coffee and leaned across to where I was sitting. She ran her palm over my hand and up my forearm, then met my eyes. "You look good, Garner. Even better than I remember."

I stared at her, empty of words.

"It's been too long since we've made love, don't you think?" she said. "I've missed it. I've missed you. Let's go upstairs together."

None of the choices concerning Sylvie had been mine to make until that moment. She was the one who decided to date me, to have Willow, to leave, to return. For the first time in years, I had the power to decide what would happen between us. As soon as I was given that power, I knew what my choice would be.

My choice was no. My choice was done.

I felt no stirring of emotion in the face of her movie-star beauty, or her hand on my arm, or her invitation to bed. I was finally able to let go of the last of the love I had for her, and all the bitterness, too.

Done.

I took a hammock ride with Sylvie Rolland once. It was full of thrills while it lasted, but just like Willow and Nora's hammock ride with Sylvie, mine ended in heartache and regret. I never want to do it again. I don't want to be chained by the memory of it any longer, either.

I removed Sylvie's hand from my arm and told her that I'd moved on. It felt like victory, to say those words and mean them. It felt like the end of a story that needed finishing.

Sylvie can continue to be in Willow's life. She can't have custody, but, fortunately for Willow and me, she doesn't want custody. I don't think she'll ever want it. She enjoys dropping in or calling or sending a package when the mood strikes her. That's the version of motherhood she prefers, and she can have it. But she can't have me. I won't simmer with anger over her anymore. Or stew with guilt.

I've carried a tremendous amount of guilt because of my affair with Sylvie and because of Robin's death. I've asked for God's forgiveness countless times. Academically, I know that He's forgiven me. However, I've never been able to forgive myself.

Tonight, here in my room, with Sylvie sleeping a floor below me and my girls sleeping in the room next to mine, I'm finally ready to release the guilt.

Done.

I'm forgiven. It's hard to believe. It doesn't make sense. It's not fair or deserved, but it *is* true. I'm forgiven.

God's grace is like a rushing river. It's far more powerful than I am. My sins don't stand a chance against it.

I've made awful mistakes, but I'm beginning to realize that God was able to use those mistakes. He's been working behind the scenes for my good all along. If I'd had my way, I wouldn't have Willow. I wouldn't have Kathleen.

Through Kathleen, God's extending ~~a second chance~~ to me. No, not a second chance. A third.

I'm thankful. I'm very thankful that God's plans for me were different than the plans I had for myself.

CHAPTER
Eighteen

Phone Message from Kathleen to Her Friend Rose

Garner didn't come to work today. I had a horrible night's sleep and now I'm sick to my stomach because I'm so worried that he's spending the day with Sylvie and that she's busy casting her spell over him.

What's happened to me, Rose? Nothing but Estée Lauder used to get me even half this emotional. Now I'm a basket case. Being in love stinks! I don't want awards or promotions or applause or a job at Estée Lauder. I just want Garner. That's all.

Handwritten Letter Slipped beneath the Door of Kathleen's Apartment

Kathleen,

I'm really sorry about last night. I had no idea that Sylvie was coming, and I apologize for the predicament that put you in.

Sylvie's leaving tomorrow so the girls and I are going to spend the day with her. I think it's important to Willow for her parents to have a friendly relationship. So I'm trying to be nice. I'm making an effort to be a good host.

We're leaving to go to the zoo soon. Since I don't want to call you at the office, I decided to write. On the way to the zoo, I'll drive by your apartment and drop this off.

I want you to know that I love you.

What I used to feel for Sylvie was a young man's love.

What I feel for you is an older, and hopefully wiser, man's love.

I acknowledge that it's a lot, to ask you to date a man with a past like mine. I've had a child out of wedlock. I've been married before. I've been marked by tragedy. I come with two little girls who will look to any future wife of mine to be their mother. I'll never move to New York. I can't. I have to stay here because it's my responsibility to run the company that carries my family name.

I'm well aware that you could date someone without as many faults. It would probably be easier on you to date someone who won't worry about you as much as I will.

You'll have to make sacrifices to be with me, Kathleen. I'm sorry for that. But if you choose to be with me anyway, I promise to love you with everything I have for as long as God lets me.

You're a gift I never expected. You've changed my life and made me believe in a future I couldn't even imagine until I met you.

I'll be home tonight. If you want, you can call me at the usual time. But I'll understand if you need a few days to think about everything I've written. Or if you decide not to call. You're free, Kathleen. You're free to choose.

—Garner

Phone Conversation between Kathleen and Garner

GARNER: Hello?

KATHLEEN: Garner.

GARNER: Kathleen?

KATHLEEN: You said I could call at the usual time.

GARNER: Are you crying?

KATHLEEN: I'm laughing and crying at the same time. Your letter! Oh my goodness, your letter.

GARNER: I wasn't sure how you'd react.

KATHLEEN: I adore your letter. I've read it one hundred times since I got home from work.

GARNER: You have?

KATHLEEN: Yes. I've committed whole sections of it to memory.

GARNER: I've been afraid . . . that you wouldn't call.

KATHLEEN: I would—very much—like to date you. Garner? You still there?

GARNER: Yes, sorry. I'm smiling too much to talk.

KATHLEEN: I'm smiling, too. When Sylvie leaves, maybe I can take you and the girls out for chocolate cake.

GARNER: Maybe I'll take you and the girls out for hot fudge sundaes.

KATHLEEN: Maybe we'll order both. Dutch treat.

Phone Message from Kathleen to Her Friend Rose

Garner loves me! Disregard my pathetic message from earlier in the day. Delete it please, and don't ever tell a soul about it.

All is right with the world, Rose. All is right with the world!

Phone Message from Kathleen to Her Mother, Margaret

Mom, can you do me a favor and sit down?

Are you sitting? Okay, everything's fine. No need to worry. I'm calling with very happy news, actually. You were right about Garner Bradford having a girlfriend. He does.

His girlfriend is me.

Which is why I wanted you to sit down.

Don't be alarmed. Don't be upset. I'm telling you this news through a message on purpose, so that you can hear it and have time to adjust to it *before* we talk. Please don't call me back for at least forty-eight hours, okay? In fact, let's just wait to talk until I see you at the country club on Saturday.

He's a wonderful man, Mom. I think, once you get to know him, that you'll like him as much as I do.

This really is good news. Yay! I'm going to stay in Shelton and date Garner and help him save Bradford Shipping.

If I don't answer my phone between now and when I see you at the country club, it's not because I've been in a car accident. It's because I'm giving you time to adjust. If you need to talk to one of your children about this, call Shane. He's wonderful. So consoling!

Love you. Bye.

Phone Message from Margaret to Her Friend Dorothy Four Days Later

Yes, it's true that Kathleen's dating Garner Bradford. He's from a well-respected family. He has an excellent job. And he's proven himself to be of good character since his first child was born.

Not to mention, he's smitten with Kathleen and he's certainly handsome. I've always favored men with light eyes.

All in all, I'm pleased. Truth be told, I've thought all along that they'd make a good match.

Card from Kathleen to Garner One Month Later

Happy birthday, Garner!

You've enriched my life in too many ways to write down. However, I feel compelled to write down at least a few.

You understand me. You accept my weaknesses and my strengths. You make me feel at home. You listen. You kiss really, really well. You're a great friend to me and a great father to your girls. You're not too shabby as CEO. And you make the best homemade pizza.

I love you. I really do.

—Kathleen

Note Tied with a Ribbon to a Solitaire Diamond Ring Two Weeks Later

I love you, Kathleen.

Will you marry me?

CHAPTER

Nineteen

Garner's Journal Entry

It's been a long time since I've written.

Kathleen and I married last summer and today, April 20, 1992, our daughter was born.

Brittany Margaret Bradford
7 pounds, 12 ounces
18 inches long

She's perfect and healthy and Kathleen is perfect and healthy and Willow and Nora, now six and four, are perfect and healthy, too. The older girls are in awe of the baby. Hopefully, they'll continue to be, at least until we bring her home from the hospital and they start resenting her.

We'll cross that bridge when we come to it.

I'm only home for a minute, to shower and pick up the things Kathleen wanted me to bring to the hospital for her. But I'm feeling sentimental and incredibly grateful, so I've hauled out my old journal.

I'm married to Kathleen.

I'm the father of three wonderful girls.

I'm the luckiest man in the world.

Work is still challenging for me. It looked for a while like our best efforts might not be enough to pull Bradford Shipping back from the edge. Change was expensive and painful. But the task force and I overhauled the company anyway, and eventually, the tide began to turn. The first quarter of this year, we posted a profit. And we just landed two huge new accounts. All without updating our computer software.

I'm laughing because Kathleen would be mad at me if she knew I'd written that. I don't want her to be mad at me. Ever, but especially not today. What Kathleen doesn't know is that I've already spoken to our staff about updating the software later this year. Her ideas about our software were right, after all. Just ahead of their time.

Fear is still challenging for me. I don't curb Kathleen's independence, but it does scare me when she goes out alone. Because she knows how I feel, she never walks or runs by herself. Still. I struggle with anxiety. Every day, I pray for Kathleen's safety and for the safety of the girls. I never take their well-being for granted. Not for a minute.

Optimism is still challenging for me. There are times when I'm terrified that Kathleen will leave. However, those times are fewer and fewer. Every day that I wake up beside her leads me to hope just a little bit more that God might give us many, many years together. Kathleen's strong and persuasive and feisty. Feisty enough, I hope, to stick with me and refuse to give up on us.

I'm desperate for the chance to grow old with Kathleen. To raise our daughters together, to celebrate holidays, to renovate Bradfordwood to its former glory, to eat chocolate cake and hot fudge sundaes together, to watch each season fade into the next.

Despite the challenges, I really am the luckiest man. I love my wife. I love my girls. And they love me. We're a family.

The future is no longer heavy and gray. The future is golden, I hope. I'm stepping into it with anticipation. Anticipation and expectancy.

"Be strong and courageous. Do not be terrified; do not be discouraged, for the Lord your God will be with you wherever you go."

-Joshua 1:9

The Bradford sisters are all grown up!
Begin the BRADFORD SISTERS ROMANCE series with
Nora's love story . . . .

True to You

Three years after a devastating heartbreak, genealogist and historical village owner Nora Bradford has decided that burying her nose in her work and her books is far safer than romance in the here and now.

Unlike Nora, former Navy SEAL John Lawson is a modern-day man, usually 100 percent focused on the present. However, when John, an adoptee, is diagnosed with an inherited condition, he's forced to dig into the secrets of his ancestry.

John enlists Nora's help to uncover the identity of his birth mother. As they work side-by-side, this pair of opposites begin to suspect that they just might be a perfect match.

FICTION WRITTEN BY BECKY WADE

True to You (BRADFORD SISTERS ROMANCE novel #1)
Undeniably Yours (PORTER FAMILY novel #1)
Meant to Be Mine (PORTER FAMILY novel #2)
A Love Like Ours (PORTER FAMILY novel #3)
The Proposal (PORTER FAMILY Christmas story #3.5)
Her One and Only (PORTER FAMILY novel #4)
My Stubborn Heart
Love in the Details

Sign Up for Becky's Newsletter

For the latest news about Becky's upcoming books, sneak peeks of yet-to-be-published chapters, and exclusive giveaways, subscribe to Becky's free quarterly e-newsletter at:

beckywade.com

Your email address will never be shared and you can unsubscribe at any time.

About the Author

Becky Wade is a California native who attended Baylor University, met and married a Texan, and settled in Dallas. She published historical romances for the general market before putting her career on hold for several years to care for her three children. When God called her back to writing, Becky knew He meant for her to turn her attention to Christian fiction. She loves writing funny, heartwarming, and inspirational contemporary romance! She has won the Carol Award, INSPY Award, and Inspirational Reader's Choice Award. To learn more, visit her website.

beckywade.com/home

Connect with Becky

You can find her on Facebook as Author Becky Wade and on Twitter, Instagram, and Pinterest as BeckyWadeWriter.